CURSE OF THE BEARS

Wild Ridge Bears Book Four

KIMBER WHITE

Nokay Press LLC

Author's Note

The Wild Ridge Bears Series have all been written so you can enjoy them as standalones with a guaranteed happily ever after. While they can be read in any order, the events within them happen chronologically and there may be spoilers with other plot threads if you read them out of order. The recommended reading order is as follows:

Lord of the Bears
Outlaw of the Bears
Rebel of the Bears
Curse of the Bears
Last of the Bears

Chapter One

RAFE

When the first man got sick, we chalked it up to bad luck. Copper mining is brutal work, even for shifters, but we're suited for it. My crew works around the clock. We don't take shifts. We stay down there until the work is done. Copper dust doesn't affect our lungs. We heal fast. Cave-ins can't break our backs. When they happen, we can dig our way out with our bare hands if we have to. If the lights go out, our eyes see well beyond the blackness.

When the second man got sick, denial set in. He was careless, maybe. He was one of the newer hires. Maybe he wasn't truly cut out for mining, bear shifter or not.

When the third man got sick, fear started to spread. The first two came from Simon Marshall's crew. As Alpha of the Marshall clan, he's a strong leader, but not the most popular. I know some of the other clan members figured maybe Simon cut corners or put his men at risk. They never said anything so bold within my hearing because they knew what I would say. Sure, Simon could be a dick, but he'd die before he put his men in danger. Every clan leader took the same oath and lived by it, including me.

Then, the first man died.

Simon made the call we all dreaded. We shut down operations across the entire ridge. To my knowledge, this hadn't been done in over a century. Wild Ridge, nestled deep in Michigan's Upper Peninsula, is one of the largest bear clan lands in the world. Our fathers and grandfathers have fought to keep it safe for hundreds of years. Until now, the threats we faced came from the outside. Other shifters wanted this place; they still do. We've fought off other clans, wolf shifters, witches, and some say even dragons back when regular men had barely figured out how to walk upright. Our mines gave us work and wealth; the ridge itself and the churning expanse of Lake Superior formed a natural barrier to the outside world that kept us well protected. But this time, the threat seemed to come from within.

This time, it felt different. I don't remember the last shifter wars. Those had happened before I was born. My father remembers, even though he was barely more than a teenager when he fought alongside the fathers of all the current clan leaders. Most of them are all dead, paving the way for my generation to take over. Simon, Bo Calvin, and Trevor Scott have all lost their fathers. I think in many ways that made it easier for them to lead their clans as Alphas. For me, Jaxon Lord, and Cullen James, our fathers are still here. Well, mine is. Cullen's was banished for trying to let outsiders onto the ridge. Jax's has gone to live in the Yukon. That just leaves me as the lone clan Alpha whose father won't quite fade away.

"Rafe!" My father pounded on my cabin door. He needn't have bothered. I sensed him the instant he left his own cabin further up the ridge. Pulling on my boots, I opened the door. Ansel, retired Alpha to the McCormack clan stood before me, his silver hair shining in the sunlight. His skin rippled near his jaw as he fought the urge to shift. It made my own bear stir. I gripped the doorknob hard, fighting back my baser instincts. When I was a much younger bear, just a hard look from my father would have been enough to bring my bear out. Now, the echo of that primal instinct remained. He still challenged me with his eyes almost every time he came here. Was I still strong enough to fend him off? Did I still deserve to wear the mantle of Clan Alpha that he'd reluctantly given up when his body started to break down?

"I know," I said, opening the door wider so Ansel could cross the threshold. "You know I know. Simon and Jax have called a clan meeting up at the longhouse. Why don't you stay here until I get back? I'll let you know if anything's been decided."

Ansel grunted as he turned on his heel and glowered at me. "This concerns me as much as it does you, son. If bears are dying on this ridge, one of ours could be next."

One of mine, I wanted to say. I bit my tongue. My father wasn't wrong that the health of the clans as a whole concerned him too. But, every time he wanted to follow me up to the longhouse at the top of the ridge for a full clan meeting, it ran the risk of weakening me in the eyes of the others. Either he was Clan Alpha or I was. If he forced the issue, he could never best me and he knew it.

"Still," I said. "We don't know what's caused this sickness. If it *is* viral, you're better off staying away from the longhouse anyway."

"You saying I'm not strong enough to fight it off?"

"I'm saying why put yourself at risk?"

My father curled and uncurled his fists at his sides. "I'm worried, Rafe. Something feels different this time."

I slowly closed my eyes and let out a long breath. Testosterone couldn't be the deciding factor on what was best for the clans.

Infuriating though he was, my father *had* been around a long damn time. We needed ideas and answers. Part of being a good Clan Alpha was putting clan interests above personal ones. Unfortunately, my father didn't always remember that.

"Fine," I said. "But you stand in the back. Do you understand? You're there for counsel only."

My father narrowed his dark eyes at me and leaned forward on one foot, closing the distance between us. When I met his gaze and held it, his nostrils flared, but he finally leaned back and gave me a slow, grim nod.

"We're wasting time," I said. Grabbing my leather jacket from a hook near the front door, I headed outside. My father fell in step behind me.

The longhouse sat on the highest point of the ridge overlooking the mining town and smaller villages that housed the members of each of the six clans who lived here. My clan lived in the southwest. We controlled access to the main entrance to the northern and southern quadrants of the mine. My claim connected with Simon Marshall's. As such, our clans had formed a sometimes uneasy alliance over the years. Lately, our mines had been the largest producers on the ridge. This fact didn't always sit well with some of the other clans, but money talks. I also knew it wouldn't always be this way. In two more years, we would likely exhaust the main vein running through both of our claims and production would focus further to the east. This meant the Lord and James claims would probably take over the richest production. But, what was good for one clan on Wild Ridge was good for us all. It's how we'd survived and thrived when other bear clans perished. Today though, we were here because what was bad for one clan was also bad for us all.

As I walked into the building with my father at my side, the air itself seemed to hold dread. I took my place at the table. The somber looks around the room weighed heavy inside of me.

"Jed Davis died last night," Trevor Scott said, hanging his head. There was no preamble. No ground rules set for what we'd discuss. Trevor had just said it all. Jed was Trevor's right-hand man and cousin. His loss would hit Trevor hard. He clenched his hands together, working them until the knuckles turned white.

"Does anyone have a count?" Jax Lord asked. "I've got three men down with the same symptoms. Shaky, fever, pox running the length of their spines."

"Four here," Cullen said. "Yesterday it was just the one, but three more of my crew came down with it this morning."

Bo Calvin dropped his head. One of his crew members, Matt Tate, was the first to fall sick. That was five days ago. "I've got five. And it makes no sense. We've isolated everyone, but it's still spreading."

"How's Matt doing?" I asked.

Bo shook his head. "No change. So, I suppose that's at least something. He hasn't gotten worse. He can't shift; he can't get out of bed."

Simon slammed his fist on the table. "I've got two men down. Pete's one of them."

"What about your boy?" My father took his place against the wall behind me. His voice was thick with contempt and accusation. Enough so that Simon growled and his bear eyes flashed dark.

Simon's five-year-old son Tad was new to the clan lands. He'd been separated from Simon at birth. Everyone at this table understood my father's implication. Simon's son was the first shifter newcomer to be allowed entry to the ridge in more than ten years.

If this sickness was being passed from bear to bear, young Tad Marshall could be the carrier.

"Now just hold on," I said, sensing the rising tension between Simon and my father. It had been coming on for months...God, for decades really. Simon's father and mine had been bitter rivals. They'd fought over everything two bears possibly could: mining rights, land, mates. My mother had chosen Ansel over Simon's father. Their feud had made things difficult on the ridge for twenty years until I finally took over as Alpha. Now, among other things, my father wanted me to keep the fight going with Simon. I had my own issues with him over the years, but it was time for old rivalries to die and new blood to take over. Getting my dad to accept that was the bitch.

"Simmer the fuck down, Ansel," I said, glaring at my dad. "It really doesn't matter a whole hell of a lot how this sickness started. It's here. It's spreading. So we deal with it."

Fire lit behind my father's eyes. He was a stubborn asshole, but he wasn't unreasonable. At least, not most of the time. Even if Simon's son brought this sickness to the ridge, he was a Marshall. He belonged here.

Cullen rapped his knuckles on the oak conference table. "Rafe's right. We figure out what's causing this. I've put a call out to the Yukon clans. So far, nobody's come down with it up there. The California clans haven't seen it either. The Russians aren't talking."

"So they know," Simon said. "We've done our duty."

"We have," Jax said. "It also means we're on our own. None of the other clans want to get involved if this thing spreads from bear to bear. I can't say I blame them. We're getting help from our contacts in the biology department at Great Lakes University. If everyone here at the table will agree to it, they're willing to do an autopsy on Jed. The blood samples we sent didn't provide any answers. This thing doesn't match any known shifter pathogens. No one's ever seen or heard of anything like it since..."

Jax's voice dropped. His gaze traveled over my shoulder and back to my dad.

"Say it," Ansel said, his voice barely more than a growl.

Simon rose to his feet. His claws came out and he dug them into the table. "You say what I think you're going to say and I'm going to finish this shit with you once and for all, old man. You think you're still tough enough to take me on?"

My own bear stirred. The challenge in Simon's eyes riled everyone at the table. I felt my father's bear roll inside of him. If he shifted here, in the middle of a council meeting, he wouldn't last five seconds. He couldn't take on six Alphas at once, most of them half his age. The baser part of me wanted to see it. But, he was still my father and part of my clan. I got to my feet and leveled a hard stare at Simon.

"Ansel doesn't speak for the McCormack clan. I do. No one's saying a damn thing about your son, Simon. He's a Marshall. He's part of the ridge. No matter what."

Grunts of assent made their way around the table. I felt my father's bear recede and he leaned back against the wall. Simon's eyes dimmed to their normal brown and he finally took his seat again.

"Fine," Dad finally spoke again. "You can all just keep up this circle jerk. Every man here is thinking the same thing. This doesn't just happen. Bears just don't start getting sick. Not unless there's witchcraft involved."

He was right. As much as I wanted to muzzle the old man, he had a handy knack for giving voice to the things no one else wanted to say.

"He's right," Simon of all people said it. It had been a witch who kept him away from his son all these years. We'd narrowly avoided a war getting him back.

Jax lowered his head. "I know we've all been thinking it. Unless Jed's autopsy comes back with something else, we have to face the fact that this is a spell."

"If it's a spell, then there's a cure," I said.

"You're going to have to kill the bitch witch who cast it," Ansel said. "Any of you boys think you've got the balls to take that on?"

"Ansel, shut up," I said, looking at him over my shoulder. "Goddammit, we're *agreeing* with you and you're still trying to pick a fight."

"Then we need a plan," Cullen said. "We need to run recon. The closest enclave of Circean witches lives in southern Ohio. That's where the witch who took Simon's kid's family came from."

"You can't face 'em head on, son," Ansel said. "You do that, shit's liable to escalate quicker than you can handle."

"I said recon," Cullen sighed. "I'll go myself."

"No," Jax yelled. "Cullen, you can't. You've got a family now. That leaves Simon out too. I'll go."

Something stirred inside me and this time it wasn't my bear. My vision seemed to tunnel and it got harder to isolate the words each man spoke. They argued. They thumped their chests and pounded their fists on the table. Simon wanted to go, but his wife was pregnant and his young son still needed him. Trevor volunteered, but his grief over Jed clouded his judgment. As their voices escalated, my mind became still and I knew what I needed to do.

"It's me," I said, rising from the table. "It's my job to go."

Ansel grabbed me by the shoulder and pressed down with all his strength. He tried to force me back into my chair. His eyes went wide with fear when he saw my face and my resolve. But, once I'd said it, everyone at the table seemed to understand the truth of my words.

"I'll go." I said it again. "I'll leave tonight. The longer we wait, the more danger we face."

"You don't even have a fucking plan," my father yelled.

I turned to face him. "Well, I'm not planning to face a coven of Circean witches head on, if that's what you're thinking. I'll go and see if I can find anything out. We need to know if this was a planned attack or just one rogue witch with an ax to grind."

"You've got nothing to prove, son!"

My vision tunneled again. The fact that he felt compelled to stand here at my back in the middle of a council meeting told everyone otherwise. My father's eyes settled when he understood my mind was made up. After that, there was nothing left to say.

I left at daybreak taking nothing more than a backpack with a change of clothes in it. I'd travel on foot and hunt along the way. I didn't even wait to say goodbye to my father or any of the others. There'd be no need. If everything went according to plan, I'd be back in a couple of days with something useful to report.

I should have known when I left that nothing would ever go according to plan again.

IT TURNS OUT WITCHES ARE EASIER TO SCENT THAN OTHER shifters. My father warned me the opposite was true. He said if a witch knows you're coming, she knows how to hide and you'll never find her until you're close enough to get your ass kicked.

On this day, this witch had no idea I was coming.

I stayed in my bear until I reached the edge of Salt Fork State Park. Following the jagged, bending banks of the Salt Fork River, I knew the Circean witches lived near Cambridge, Ohio in the foothills of the Appalachian Mountains. Centuries ago, some of our people lived there too. Not anymore. In fact, the further south I traveled, I sensed the absence of shifters in this wilderness. It made my bones turn cold.

I'd made camp in a natural cave formed by two rocky outcroppings and a large maple tree upended by the roots, probably during the last big storm. I could still smell the charge in the decaying bark. I slept deep, waking only when sunlight stabbed through the leafy canopy above. My bear stirred, sensing rabbit and smaller prey ducking out behind the bushes to the east of me. Stretching, I got my legs under me and found my backpack. I dressed quickly, eager to get the chill out of my limbs. Still early spring, the sun warmed my back, but a glittering frost had settled over the forest floor.

I heard her before I saw her. Ducking low, I pressed my back against the solid bark of a tall oak tree. She chanted something. A spell perhaps? I couldn't recognize the words. The hair prickled along my spine as I caught a whiff of ozone. Scanning the horizon, I couldn't see a cloud in the sky. Whatever I scented, it was coming from the witch, not the woods. I turned to face her, keeping my body shielded by the thickest part of the tree.

She stunned me. With delicate hands and long fingers, she gathered twigs and sticks, wrapping them with strands of sweet grass.

She set them aside and rubbed her hands together. At first, I thought to warm them. Then, I saw a faint blue spark crackle between her palms. It dazzled me and seemed to infuriate her. She turned and for the first time, I could see her face.

She had a hard, dark beauty that I imagined few appreciated. Not conventionally pretty, she had a long nose, high cheekbones and thick, dark brows with a natural arch that gave her a look of permanent wonder. Her black hair fell long and straight, well past her shoulders shielding her oval-shaped face. With her olive skin and pale green eyes, she seemed a blend of dozen ethnicities.

My inner bear flared to life. I gripped the rough bark of the tree shielding me, digging my fingers deep until my claws sprang free. I slowly closed my eyes and focused on breathing. There were no shifters in these parts. Maybe not for generations. She didn't sense me. I wasn't supposed to be here.

She chanted something, her voice taking on a sultry quality as her head fell back, exposing the long column of her throat. She stood, raising her slender arms above her head. She wore a thin, white dress that looked homespun. It hung loosely off her shoulders, dropping to one side when she brought her arms back down, exposing the ample swell of her left breast. Clapping her hands together, she produced a thin blue spark between them. Her voice rose, singing words I still couldn't understand, until I did.

"Motherfucker!" she yelled at the sky.

I brought my hand to my mouth to stifle a laugh. Whatever spell she tried to cast didn't work the way she wanted. She curled her hand into a fist and drove it into the nearest tree. Crying out as she drew blood, every protective instinct inside me roared to life and drove me to my knees.

I don't remember moving or even making a sound, but I must have. The scent of her blood made my own roar in my ears. I couldn't see straight. I remember taking one staggering step to the side. She heard me. Her emerald eyes locked with mine and before I could even register her movement, that blue light shot from her fingertips again and hit me dead center in the chest.

My breath left me and my limbs went stiff as I fell to the ground and smashed my head on a rock.

Chapter Two

TALIA

One hour earlier...

It was supposed to tingle, I think. At least, it was supposed to...*something*. But, when I planted my fingers into the cold, wet earth, it just felt...well...cold and wet.

"Come on, Mother Gaia," I whispered. "Give me something to go on here."

I closed my eyes. I *did* feel the presence all around me. The roots beneath my feet teemed with life. They connected every living organism in these woods, including me. When one tree dies, the others take its nutrients. When one of *us* dies, we leave something of ourselves behind too. I drew on it. I let the crisp, cool air fill my lungs and thought of Marjorie. In the stillness, her breath kissed my bare shoulder. I might have imagined it all, but I chose not to think so.

It was such a simple spell. I cupped the tiny, wilted wildflower in my palm as I slid my free hand further into the earth. Life shifted beneath me as I unsettled an earthworm or a roly-poly or some other fat-bodied critter.

I wasn't asking for much from any of them. Just a tiny spark of healing energy to flow through them to me and into the brown leaves of the flower. I'd give it back when I planted the flower in the earth near the hundred-year-old maple tree two feet in front of me. Such a small gift, but it would prove my worth. I could do this. I *had* to do this. Otherwise, there was no point trying to go home.

My palms started to sweat and I took it as a good sign. When my toes went numb, I thought that was better still. Then, my eyes started to water and the earth warmed beneath my fingertips.

I was afraid to move, afraid to breathe even. This was it. The rapture. Grandma Torre told me it would feel like this.

"Don't try to force it," she'd said. "Let it come to you. We don't take. We enable. We facilitate. You're a conduit, Talia, nothing more. Control comes later. Just make yourself known to the Source. It'll do the rest."

"But what if the Source doesn't want anything to do with me?" I'd asked. God, it had been so long ago since I'd even dared to ask her those questions.

At nineteen, I was so far past declaring to the Source, nobody in my family liked to talk about it. Maybe I was that rare dud in the Lear family line. My father would blame my mother's side. My mother wasn't here to blame anyone, so Grandma Torre would do it for her. She'd say my father muddled things by marrying my mother in the first place. She'd say it with such conviction that anyone who didn't know better would take it as gospel. Except two things undercut her logic.

First, my father's sister had been one of the most powerful and deadly witches anyone had seen in generations. I shuddered at the memory of just how fierce that power had been. It had been strong enough to turn her away from the light. My aunt. We were forbidden to even speak her name now. The shame of her sins had stained my whole family. Last year, I'd been called to help bring her down when we realized she was too far gone to save. I had no power of my own, and the coven elders thought being near her might help me declare once and for all. That, and they needed my blood tie to her. They used it to stop her. They used it to kill her. I closed my eyes and tried to shut out the memory. I was nothing like my aunt. Nothing.

My sister Marjorie was the second thing that disproved my grand-mother's claim about the Lear line. Marjorie might have been just as powerful as our aunt. Or, she would have been if she hadn't died in a car accident when she was twelve years old.

It had been so easy for Marjorie. She was just three years older than me, but I remember sitting beside her as we walked these same trails in the winding woods out past Freedom Road. Before I understood who and what we were, I thought she was Snow White or some other fairytale princess. With just a flick of her finger or the lilt in her voice, she seemed able to talk to any living thing. She said even the trees themselves told her things. What those things were, I never knew. Grandma Torre said Marjorie had been the youngest Circean witch to declare herself to the Source in more than two centuries.

I have no idea how she knew that. There's no written registry or census that I've ever heard of. Grandma Torre just says these things and no one ever questions it. Every time she does, it's in me to point out that Marjorie's connection to the Source hadn't been enough to give her the power to stop what happened to her.

So for that, what the hell good was any of it? Marjorie still died in the middle of the road, her body crumpled and broken, her hand reaching for the soft earth and the woods beyond.

I felt something.

The wildflower moved in my hand though the air was still. Afraid to breathe, I opened a wary eye and looked at it. The purple petals curled inward and browned. My heart thundered in my chest and I dug the fingers of my left hand deeper into the ground. I felt something move there too. Slowly, I pulled the clump of earth out of the ground and uncurled my other fist. As the wildflower died in one hand, a fat, black beetle flipped to its back, waved its spindly legs in the air, and died right along with the flower. I wrapped the flower in twigs and sticks, desperate for *something* to happen. I even said the healing incantation in Latin, as if that made any difference. A tiny blue spark arched between my fingers. Just enough to piss me off but not enough to control. I curled my fist and punched the damn maple tree.

"Motherfucker!" I yelled at the sky and threw both the beetle and the flower at the maple. I had nothing to show for my efforts except sweat down my back and black earth under my fingernails. Burying my face in my hands, I pushed back my tears of frustration. I looked up toward the sky. The waving branches of the forest canopy seemed to mock my failure.

Grandma Torre's last words to me before I left this time stung me. She told me to stay out here until I declared once and for all. If it didn't happen, she'd told me not to bother to come home. She'd said I'd been coddled too long and it was time to sink or swim. This time, my father didn't argue with her. His cold, stern look as they watched me leave seared in my memory.

Then, something happened.

Thunder rumbled through the trees. It seemed to bubble up from the ground beneath me. But that's not how thunder works. Heat traveled up my spine until it felt like molten metal. My vision dimmed. Something moved through the trees a few yards ahead of me. Whatever it was, it was big and bold and headed straight for me.

"Prohibere!" Instinct took over. For the past three days, I'd tried to call every living thing to me. In the span of a heartbeat, I wanted nothing more than to drive whatever it was away.

The fevered pulse along my spine spread, following a liquid path along my arms. I didn't move. I didn't think. When the shadow loomed before me, my feet left the ground. The heat inside me radiated out in great, roping arcs of blue light.

I didn't command it. I didn't control it. It moved through me. The Source.

With the impact of a shotgun blast, the lightning poured out of me and into the shadow. Then the shadow took shape and became flesh. Or maybe, it was flesh to begin with, but I never saw that. Not until after it was over.

When the heat dissipated, my knees buckled and I fell to the ground. Sweat poured down my back and I couldn't seem to make my lungs work.

He groaned but couldn't seem to move. Using the maple tree to steady me, I carved my fingertips into the bark and pulled myself to my feet. Taking a staggering step forward, I stood over him.

"Oh, God," I whispered. He was huge, wild, and beautiful. I blinked hard, trying to get my brain to register what my eyes saw. His muscled thighs wrapped in weathered jeans looked about as big as the damn tree trunk I leaned against. He wore a faded blue flannel shirt with the sleeves rolled up revealing well-muscled forearms covered in a dusting of dark hair.

I hadn't knocked him out. He stared at me with furious dark eyes. He had a full beard and my eyes traveled to his sensual mouth, parted slightly as if he were trying to speak...or more likely, to yell at me.

"I'm sorry," I whispered. I reached for him, but curled my fists as his eyes widened.

"Right," I said. "Right. Maybe don't touch you just yet. Can you move? Can you get up?"

He moaned. The deep timbre of his voice vibrated through me, making my skin crackle again. I rubbed my palms against the front of my dress, trying to get the tingle out of them.

Real thunder rumbled in the sky, followed by the first fat drops of rain. He flinched as one landed on the bridge of his nose and made a slow trail down his cheek. Lightning crackled.

"Shit, that was quick," I said. Had I caused that? I supposed it didn't really matter now. The bigger problem was the guy still didn't seem able to move.

The wind kicked up as the gathering storm moved fast and furious. It was dangerous to be out here now among the trees. My tingling fingers punctuated my thoughts.

"Fucking hell," I said, remembering Grandma Torre's words. "I'm a conduit."

"What?" He spoke. His voice came out as a choked whisper and he hissed as he tried to lift his neck. His skin rippled and his eyes went almost black. A cold fear passed through me, but I couldn't name it. Something inside me told me to run, but I pushed it aside.

"We're not safe out here," I said. Even as I spoke, my hair started to rise in charged wisps. "Dammit. I *am* a conduit."

Lightning split the sky, spearing straight into a towering oak about twenty yards away from us. The branches smoldered.

The guy's eyes went wide with fear and he tried to reach for me, recognizing the danger we were in. We had to get out of here. The lightning seemed to be looking for me.

"Come on!" I yelled.

Fear and guilt made me reach for him. This guy just had the shit luck of hiking right in my path when the Source decided to find me. For his trouble, I'd curdled his spine and made him a target for the storm. Some back corner of my brain told me to leave him anyway. But, I couldn't. When the second bolt of lightning struck a hundred yards to the south, I made up my mind for good.

I lunged for him, pulling his arm around my shoulder. The instant my skin touched his, fire lit within me once again.

"Not bloody now!" I yelled at the sky.

I don't know how I did it. It shouldn't have been possible. He had to outweigh me by at least a hundred pounds. But something happened when we touched. It was if a new spark ran from him to me. Fresh panic poured through me when I realized his legs didn't work. He could barely hold up his own weight. Without me, he'd be helpless against the elements.

As lightning hit a third time, the ground itself seemed to catch fire.

"We have to go!" I screamed. "This way!"

We moved together. The Source moved through me, giving me the strength to hold him up. We dodged falling branches and ruts in the earth as I led him to safety. My tiny cabin in the woods would hopefully give us just enough shelter. That is if the lightning didn't hit it too.

My feet must have touched the ground, though I didn't feel it. Staggering, we reached the little log cabin tucked into a clearing beyond the cedar trees. I let go of him and shoved my shoulder into the door. It opened and we spilled into the one-room cabin together.

I shut the door behind us and found the latch just as a final bolt of lightning hit a tall pine just twenty feet away.

We were drenched. My dress clung to me like a second skin and I drew my arms around me shivering. I had a small kerosene lamp on the fireplace mantle and I lit it while he shook the water from his hair. Warm light flickered against the walls and I set the lamp down on the small wooden table in the center of the room.

"Are you okay?" I asked, taking a tentative step toward him. He was on his feet, but propped against the door.

Chilled to the bone, my teeth rattled inside my head. I smoothed my hair away from my face. It stuck to my fingers and I tried to shake that out too. He turned toward me and tried to step into the light. His legs gave out again. Without me holding onto him, his strength left him. He was hurt worse than I thought. I held the lamp forward and looked at him.

A shock went through me, more potent than the lightning. Why hadn't I sensed it before? Why hadn't I paid attention?

He straightened his shoulders and tried to pull himself up to his full height. He couldn't do it, but even slumped on the ground, I was struck by the size of him. God, he had to be at least six foot five. Maybe I'd thought it was a trick of the light before, but this time there could be no doubt. His eyes went black as he looked at me. A muscle jumped in his jaw as he tried to get to his feet again.

"Prohibere," I whispered. My fingertips crackled and his eyes widened.

"Oh, no you don't," he said, his voice rippled along the tiny hairs at the back of my neck. "You keep those hands where I can see them, witch."

I shook my head. He couldn't know what I was. Except, he did. Of course he did. I'd been so stunned by what happened I hadn't paid close enough attention.

"How did you do that?" he asked, his voice dropping low. His words came out as a growl and I realized how close he was to doing just that.

"Do what?"

"You picked me up. How the hell did you have the strength to do that?"

I opened my mouth then clamped it shut. I knew the answer but couldn't voice it to myself, let alone him. It was the Source. I had *declared*. Even as I thought it, my phone vibrated in my back pocket. I didn't need to pull it out to see who it was. The thing would blow up now. Everyone in my family would have felt what happened by now.

"You could have killed me," he said, falling forward. He caught himself with his hands. His back bunched and rippled and my heart damn near exploded with fear. "Is that what you were trying to do?"

"No," I said, taking a step back. Then, "No, no, no, no, no!"

He was quicker than I was even on his hands and knees. Of course he was. He grabbed me by the wrists and pulled me toward him, trying to drag me to the ground. As if I'd needed any other proof of who and what he was, he provided it with the low, rumbling growl that went through his body as he touched me.

He knew me for what I was. A witch. A threat. It registered in his bones the same way it did for me. He wasn't a man. He was a bear.

Not even the lightning could do me any good now.

Chapter Three

I WRENCHED my wrist free of him and staggered back toward the opposite wall. The lamp fell from my grip but landed upright on the ground. His head swung low; his breath came out in a chuff as his nostrils flared. Fur sprouted along his forearms and his finger-nails turned black.

"Don't you dare," I said, raising my hands. I didn't think I had enough strength left to zap him again, but he didn't need to know that.

His eyes widened, focusing on my fingertips. He was afraid of me. Afraid of the power that might come out of me if I decided to aim it at him again. He took a breath. When he exhaled, the fur receded and his claws retracted back to human hands.

"Just stay where you are," I said. My voice cracked, and my throat felt dry as sandpaper. Rain pelted the thin roof of the cabin.

It took everything in me not to scream. It was bad enough that my heart thundered so loudly in my chest that I was sure he could hear it too. He was a bear. A bear!

"I know what you are," I said.

"What do you think I am?"

"I didn't mean to hurt you." I realized how important it was that he believe me. It was the truth. I hadn't been trying to hurt him. He'd just startled me. I just had to hope he had more human than beast inside of him and could listen to reason.

He almost got his legs beneath him again, but then took a faltering step backward, staggered sideways, and leaned against the doorframe. I thought he had recovered. He hadn't. He looked at me with those dark bear eyes. I could sense the beast beneath him. He was simmering just below the surface. It was a beast. Carnal. Primal. Wild. He wanted something from me. Blood? I could sense his hunger. It almost felt like my own. It was the Source. It had to be. Energy still crackled from my fingertips. I wanted to touch him. I wanted to feel the connection that he had to the beast. I craved it. It scared me.

"I know what you are."

"You keep saying that," he said. He shook the rain from his head again and stopped trying to stand. He settled against the door-frame and punched his fist against the wall. Something flickered behind his eyes. I don't know how he had the strength to keep the bear in check. Yes, I did. It was me. What I did to him. Oh, God. What I did to him. I had weakened him. I had hurt him. Me. A witch. I couldn't be just like my aunt. But, I felt her presence somehow. I knew with absolute certainty what she would have done. She would have moved in for the kill. A flare of alarm went through me as I realized I had my own inner beast to quell.

"What were you doing out there?" I asked.

A low, rumbling laughter rippled through him. He was still weak.

That was plain. I think it's the only thing that kept him from trying to tear my limbs right out of their sockets. I knew I should be grateful for that. But I wasn't. What I had done, what I had almost done. If I had lost control and let the energy flow through me with the strength that I knew it had, I might have killed him. Then we would be in a whole heap of shit that I didn't know how to undo.

"What are you going to do to me?" I kept my back pressed against the opposite wall. I put as much distance between the two of us as I could in the small confines of the cabin. Thunder boomed outside and flashes of lightning lit the cabin walls, leaving jagged, blue streaks. The full weight of what I had actually done to this man, this bear, started to settle over me. He still couldn't use his legs.

"What am I going to do to *you*? Are you serious? Look at me!"

"I'm sorry," I said. "Are you in pain?"

"What was that?" he asked. "With your fingertips. How did you do that?"

I bit my tongue. I'd said too much already. He wasn't supposed to be here. No shifters of any kind were supposed to be here. Salt Fork was no man's land. Well, no shifter's land, anyway. This was witch country. Everyone knew that. I knew I should let him go. That was probably the wisest course of action. The longer I stayed in his presence, the longer I stood here and talked to him, the more he could find out about me. I didn't know how shifters worked. But I know that he could smell me and track me and do all those other icky things that shifters do. For all I knew he wasn't alone. Holy shit! What if he wasn't alone?

Reason started to fly out of my head. In its place emotion and more crackling energy went through me in waves. His eyes widened. It never occurred to me that he could see any change in me or any beast inside of me the way I could see in his eyes. Clearly he could. If it weren't for the wall at his back, or the weakness in his legs from the thunderbolt that I just shot through him, maybe he would have run. It would've been better for both of us if he did. This was bad, and it was getting worse by the second. Shifters and witches don't mix. Me being in the same room with him, let alone talking to him, let alone *touching* him violated just about every covenant that Circean witches live by. A new fear settled over me. If I *did* let him go, he might go for help. He might bring more bears back here to retaliate for what I'd done. I took a steadying breath and stood up. I knew instinctively that how I handled the next few minutes might mean the difference between both of us surviving and war.

I moved toward him. His eyes followed me and his back stiffened, but he didn't make any other move to grab me.

"I asked you a question," I said, making my voice hard. I suddenly wished I were taller. Even sitting, he barely had to look up to keep his eyes locked with mine. "What's a bear doing this far south?" I spat out the word "bear" as if it tasted bad in my mouth.

He set his jaw and rolled his eyes at me. So far, my attempt to seem imposing fell flat. I raised my hands and closed my eyes. Now that I'd done it once, it was so much easier. God, why had this been so hard up until now? Energy coursed through me. My fingertips heated. When I opened my eyes again, sparks danced between the webbing of my fingers. If my words didn't intimidate him, my blue fire sure as hell did.

He pressed his head against the door and put his own hands up in a gesture of surrender. "Don't," he said. "Put those away before you hurt yourself."

Unbidden rage flooded through me. I didn't mean to do it, but a ball of blue light shot through my fingertips and hit the door two inches above his head. He dodged sideways just in time and nearly toppled over. My pulse spiked and it got hard to breathe. I clenched my fists and dug them into my side as heat raced through me. Grandma Torre's words filled my head.

Control comes later.

"Jesus Christ," he shouted. He struggled to stand, but his legs gave out yet again. He'd been doing a hell of a lot better controlling the rage inside of him than I apparently could. He wasn't anymore. A growl ripped from his throat and those bear eyes of his went coal black. His nose twitched and he bared his teeth.

I took a step back, then another until I pressed my back against the opposite wall again. No matter what, I couldn't get that close to him again until I had a firmer grip on the power that flowed through me. If one burst of energy crippled him, a second might kill him.

My phone rang again, startling the both of us. I held up a silencing finger and answered it. The last thing I needed was Grandma Torre or my father sending anyone out here to look for me.

"Hi, Dad," I said, turning so the bear couldn't see my face.

"Talia, are you all right?" My father's voice sounded unnaturally high.

"I'm okay," I said. "There's a storm, though. I'm going to stay in the cabin until it passes."

"You'd better," he answered. "You finally did it though, didn't you? I didn't just imagine that?"

I bit my lip and looked back at the bear. He'd crossed his arms in front of him and shot me a look of exasperation. I held up a finger again and widened my eyes at him. He was smart enough to realize me calling for reinforcements from my people would be just as bad for him as if he called a clan of bears after me.

"You didn't imagine it," I said, careful to parse my words. The bear knew enough already. Hell, I shuddered to think what my aunt would have said if she were still alive. She probably would have told me to kill him where he sat. She'd been way too radical, though. She thought all shifters deserved to die. The rest of us honored the truce. Bears kept to themselves, and we kept to ourselves.

Until today, that was. Now I'd used magic to injure a bear and violated that truce. I struggled to keep the tremor of fear out of my voice as I talked to my father. "I'll be home soon. I just want to wait out the storm and collect myself. I promise, if anything else happens, I'll call you. I'll tell you all about it when I get home."

"Okay, Tal. I trust you. And I'm proud of you. Your mother would be too."

My throat closed past a hard lump that formed there. He never talked about my mother. Not ever. It hurt him too much. I closed my eyes and fought off tears threatening to form. Not now. I couldn't afford to get emotional. Not when I had a keyed up bear shifter at my back liable to tear me apart if he got his legs working again. And if he *didn't* get them working again, I'd have to figure out a way to get rid of him without starting a new witch-shifter war to boot.

"I'll talk to you later. I just want to rest for a little while." I clicked off before he could say anything else that might make me cry. Then, I turned back to the bear.

"Big day for you, I take it?" he said. His voice had that hard edge again. He'd recovered from the lightning bolt he'd almost taken to the face. That simmering rage cracked inside of me again. It was part of my DNA to hate his kind, but something else was happening too. I felt oddly drawn to him. I kept my fists clenched and once again moved closer. Now that I'd tasted the power of the Source, I could sense a different power coming from him. God help me, I wanted to feel it.

"You didn't answer my question," I said. "What are you doing in Salt Fork? Your kind doesn't belong here."

He shot me a devastating smirk and fresh heat flared through me. I sank slowly down until I squatted in front of him, putting us at eye level. Judging the span of his reach, I put just enough distance between us so I could defend myself if he made a move toward me.

"I took a wrong turn," he said, resting the back of his head against the doorframe. He winced as he lifted one heavy leg with his hands and readjusted his position.

"Does it hurt?" The question flew out of me. My eyes flicked toward his. A new flash of lightning illuminated the room as the storm outside changed direction. It still wasn't safe to go out there.

"Yeah," he said. "It hurts."

I dropped my head and sat down hard. I crossed my legs in front of me and rested my chin in my palm.

"I'm sorry. I swear I wasn't trying to hurt you. I didn't even realize you were there."

He cocked his head to the side and regarded me. God, this bear had a way of looking straight through me that both unsettled me and sent zinging heat straight up my spine that didn't seem to have anything to do with the magic.

"So, is this permanent?" He winced as he tried to shift his weight again. On instinct, I reached out to him, then froze, drawing my hand slowly back. The truth was, I had no earthly idea whether my carelessness had paralyzed this man for good. Fear and guilt spread through me with the knowledge that if he *had* been just a normal man and not a shifter, my blast might very well have killed him.

"No," I lied, hoping like crazy that it *was* true. If I'd paralyzed him for good, there was no way I could keep the others from finding out. "It's just going to take some time to wear off, that's all."

"How much time?" His voice took on a hard edge that made the hair stand up on the back of my neck.

"A day. Maybe two. Or it could wear off in a few hours. It just depends on how strong you are."

His eyes narrowed and he slammed his head against the door. "Why do I get the distinct feeling you are full of shit?"

I took in a hard breath then blew it out. I got up and started to pace. Energy crackled in my palms, so I kept my fists clenched tight. "Look, you brought this on yourself. You crossed over into *our* lands, not the other way around. Remember that. If it weren't for me, you'd have been zapped to a crisp out there."

"If it weren't for *you*? Witch, if it weren't for you none of this would have happened at all! Now, are you going to help me, or what? Clearly you have no idea how to do that on your own or you already would have. So either unzap me or get back on the phone and tell your daddy to come help you."

A ball of blue fire shot from my palm and sparked harmlessly against the stone hearth. I whirled back to face the bear. His eyes flashed dark with a predatory fury that called to something wild inside of me. I don't remember making a conscious decision to go to him, but before I could stop myself, I slid to my knees in front of him and grabbed him by the shirt. The Source surged through me and I lifted him off his feet. He took a halting step forward but couldn't control his movements.

Oh, God. He was powerful. The heat coming off of him enveloped me. The temptation to tap into the magic inside of him made my knees weak and pulse race. My own power emboldened me and allowed me to move him easily. Had he been at full strength, he might have been able to stop me. Part of me wanted him too. Some preternatural instinct sparked deep inside of me. Even though I knew he was my enemy, I wanted to draw from him.

I took two strides forward and heaved him onto the cot in the corner of the cabin. He landed with a thud and the cot's metal frame creaked in protest, but it held. I meant to back away, but he gripped my elbows and held me against him.

"What did you *do* to me, witch?" he growled.

"Nothing you didn't deserve, bear." I spat back.

Liquid heat poured through me, spreading beneath my breastbone then settling lower down. The bear's eyes sparked as the beast stirred inside of him. His breath became my breath. His pulse echoed my own. I shouldn't have touched him. I knew it. But, as his flesh seared mine, something ancient came to life inside of me. At first, I didn't have a name for it, but as his dark eyes held mine and heat pulsed in my core, I knew it for what it was.

Desire.

His eyes widened and a low noise rumbled through him, making the cabin walls vibrate just like the thunder outside. He felt something pass between us too. I squeezed my eyes shut, trying to drive it out. But, when I opened them again, I couldn't help but focus on the way his luscious lips parted as he held them so close to mine.

God, I wanted him. I wanted to kiss him. Just once. I wanted to taste the kind of power he possessed that let him shift into the beast. Instead, he blinked first and let me go. I took a step backward and got my feet under me again. I wiped my mouth with the back of my hand, trying to drive out the imagined heat of his lips on mine.

This was impossible. He was the sworn enemy of my people. And yet, the simple touch of his skin to mine ignited something dark and deep in both of us. Black magic. Danger. That's all it was. It was just an adrenaline rush from my first brush with the Source.

"Just, *stay* here," I gasped. "Rest. If your legs come back in the middle of the night, then do us both a favor and leave. Go back to wherever you came from and I won't tell *my* people I found you here."

Damn him. He smirked at me. "And if my legs don't come back?"

I put a hand to my forehead. Thunder cracked again and it felt like the walls were closing in on me. God, if his legs *didn't* come back, then what the hell would I do about him?

"Then, I'll...I'll check on you in the morning."

That now familiar energy sizzled in my palms. It rose up within me. I had to get out of here and put some distance between us. I was still so new to this degree of magic. If I stayed here another second and let him touch me again, there was no telling what might happen.

"Well, then, sleep tight, witch," he said. He hooked his fingers behind his head and settled back on the mattress. God, how could he be so smug when I felt like I was coming apart at the seams?

"Don't press your luck, bear," I said. Then I turned, slammed the door behind me, and headed back out into the storm.

Chapter Four

RAFE

She had no idea the kind of willpower it took not to go after her when she slammed the door and left me there. Thunder echoed the driving urge inside of me, making the walls of her tiny cabin vibrate. The storm raged again, almost fierce enough to break this place apart.

I brought my hands up and covered my face, willing the trembling in my fingers to subside. God. Her scent was all over me. The thrill of it went straight to my cock. I slammed a fist against the pine walls. The bear churned inside of me, struggling to come out. Her magic called to mine and left me shuddering in its wake.

It wasn't supposed to be like this. She was a witch. I was a bear. Her kind had done more damage to mine than humans ever could. How the hell had I been so careless as to let a witch find me? But, the instant I caught her scent and laid eyes on her, I just flat out couldn't turn away. She compelled me in ways that made no sense. But, the minute our skin touched, her nature stirred me and told me something impossible.

She was an Anam Cara. A bear's mate.

Except she couldn't be. A witch? It had to be a trick. It had to be some aftereffect of her sorcery scrambling my brains or parts lower down. I rubbed my jaw hard and threw my legs over the side of the cot.

Slowly, I rose. My legs felt a little shaky at first, but my steps came easy after the first one. It remained to be seen whether my deception was brilliant or stupid. That first jolt of power from her fingertips knocked me on my ass and damn near stopped my heart. She'd moved faster than any human woman should have, even if she were a witch. But, she didn't seem to have any control over the power she wielded. She tried to cover, but I knew it came as much as a shock to her as it had to me. Better to feign helplessness than risk her thinking I was a threat. The truth was, if she'd zapped me again, she just *might* have been able to do real damage.

Now, she was scared. She tried to play it off, but I could see it in her eyes and sense it in the way her pulse fluttered when she touched me. The witch was right that I had no business on Salt Fork lands. Getting caught by her had been way too careless. But, now that I had, I might just be able to use it to my advantage. Sure, I shouldn't have been anywhere near this place, but she struck first. If she was smart, she'd have to worry what could happen if I decided to call down the rest of the clans for payback. She could have called on her people for help when her father phoned, but she didn't. It had to mean something. Maybe I could use that somehow.

I damn near jumped out of my skin when my own phone rang in my back pocket. Looking out the window for any sign of her, I clicked off the ringer and pressed it to my ear.

"Yeah," I answered.

"It's Bo."

I pressed my forehead against the rain-pelted window. Thunder rolled, shaking the glass in the frame. I didn't want to ask the natural question. Bo had said all of two words, but his grim tone told me more than I wanted to know.

"How bad is it?" I finally said, squeezing my eyes shut to brace for the news.

"Rafe, it's getting worse. Matt Tate and Pete Marshall died this morning. We have ten new cases all up and down the ridge. Three of them are from your crew."

My legs felt weak again. I pressed my hand to the small of my back and stretched it. The lingering tingle of the witch's touch stiffened my bones.

"Dammit. How's Simon taking it?"

Bo let out a hard breath. "He's scared, Rafe. No one's ever seen him like this. God, I've been so damn jealous of him and Jax and Cullen for finding mates. Now, I'm just glad I'm still a bachelor and don't have to worry about children of mine falling sick. Whatever this is, we can't figure out how to fight it."

"Any word from our people at Great Lakes University?"

"Nothing good," Bo answered. "The labs on Jed's autopsy didn't show anything. They can see the effect of this thing, but don't have anything new on a potential cause. We both know what that means."

I pressed my fingers between the grooves in the pine walls. Whoever had built this place knew what he was about. The logs fit tightly together; I couldn't find so much as a millimeter of a gap anywhere along the southern wall.

"It means Ansel's probably right," I said, my voice sounding hollow to my own ears. Until that moment, I hadn't realized how badly I wanted to prove my father wrong. But, with each negative test from the shifter-friendly doctors and biologists we had working on this thing, the more likely the cause was mystical.

"Yeah," Bo answered. "Dammit, Rafe. You know I hate this as much as you do. Please tell me you've got a lead. Things are getting desperate up here. With you gone, Ansel's more riled up than ever."

I pushed myself away from the window and started to pace. "Let me guess, he's already calling for retaliation."

Bo let out a bitter laugh. "Pretty much."

"He's out of his old, damn mind. Until we know for sure what we're dealing with, it makes no sense to fly off half-cocked. I'm so sick of him throwing history in our faces. For the time being, this is a Wild Ridge problem. If our people are getting sick, the last thing we need is to charge off after a coven of witches."

"I hear you. For now, the rest of the council agrees with you. But, I can't promise you for how long. Simon's taking Pete's death really hard. He blames himself. Thank *God* he's got himself a mate now. She's managed to keep him calm. What have you found out?"

I bit my lip and kept on pacing. I don't know why I didn't come straight out and tell Bo what had happened since I got down here. My very first encounter with a witch and she damn near killed me. What more proof did I need that her kind had the means and motive to do my kind harm? But, I couldn't be my father. If this was a new Witch War, we had to play it smart. We needed a hell of a lot more information before we reacted.

"I came across a witch," I said. The instant the words flew out of my mouth, a strange, protective urge flared. *My witch!* I wanted to say. Except it made no sense.

"And?"

I sat back down on the cot, hung my head, and pressed my fingers against my forehead. "And that's about it. I caught her alone. She might be useful."

"Good," Bo said. "So what's your plan? You know what Ansel would say."

That protective urge rose up hard. My bear stirred and I had to loosen my grip on the phone before I crushed it. Yes. I knew what Ansel would say. He'd have me drag the witch right back to Wild Ridge and threaten her within an inch of her life for information.

"Yeah. I know what Ansel would have me do. I'm going to try a softer approach first. The last goddamn thing we need is to bring down the wrath of her entire coven if I spook her too soon. I need a day or two. I've got the makings of a plan."

"Anything you wanna share with me, brother?" Bo's voice took a hard edge I didn't like.

"Not yet." I don't know why I didn't want to say more. Hell, maybe that girl scrambled my brains along with my spine when she zapped me. It occurred to me if a witch's curse was indeed making our people sick, I'd just exposed the hell out of myself. Still, every instinct in me told me there was something more to her. She was different. She seemed just as scared of me as I should have been of her. No matter what, she was the best lead I had and I wasn't keen on admitting to Bo or anyone else how quickly she'd managed to get the upper hand on me.

"Well, I suppose it goes without saying, but I'm going to anyway. Be careful down there. I know we decided sending more than just one of us into witch territory was too risky. But, anything happens, you put out a call. I mean it, Rafe. We can't lose you to this."

"I appreciate that. I'll watch my back."

Bo went silent. The skies started to clear and I went to the window again. She was out there somewhere. I could still sense her. Wherever she'd gone, it seemed her mood was calmer. I didn't think the girl had the power to control the weather, but she'd sure as hell done something.

"I'll check back in with you in a day or two," I said to Bo. "In the meantime, just tell the others I'm close enough to maybe find out some shit one way or another. I won't come back empty-handed. If anything changes up there, you let me know, okay? Keep me updated on what's happening with my crew."

"You bet," Bo said. "Do what you can."

I nodded, then clicked off. Thunder rumbled outside once again. It suited my mood. I wanted to hunt. I opened the cabin door and stood in the pelting rain. Drawing in a great breath, I scented small pray to the east and something larger a few hundred yards to the south. It was a doe with her twin spring fawns. My bear roused. More than anything, I needed to shift. The girl's magic still burned through me.

She'd done something to me. It was more than just the temporary jolt to my legs. She'd called forth the deepest magic inside of me as she struggled to contain her own. My eyes snapped open and I scanned the tree line. She was out there. Not close, but my pulse quickened as I caught a whiff of her scent. It was clean and sweet, but held a hint of something darker...intoxicating. As the moon rose, a wild dog howled in the distance. But, I knew I was the most dangerous thing in these woods tonight.

I went back to the cot and waited. I told Bo I had the makings of a plan, and I did. The trouble was, I couldn't figure out if it was brilliant or ridiculous. But, every instinct I had told me the witch was telling the truth. She hadn't meant to attack me. So, I'd let her be scared. I'd let her think she'd hurt me more than she had. The more time I spent with her, maybe I could win her trust and she'd let something slip. It wasn't much, but at least it was something. If that didn't work, I could always throw her over my shoulder and head north.

God. The instant that vision came into my brain, my senses short-circuited. I imagined the feel of her strong legs kicking against me and the swell of her supple ass as I held her in place. She'd taste so sweet if I kissed her. There'd been a moment when she used her magic to throw me on the bed that I sensed desire flooding through her. It made her cheeks flush and her nipples peak. It had taken everything in me not to crush my lips to her and taste her sweetness.

"Son of a bitch," I said, fisting the thin wool blanket. "It's a spell. It's got to be her damn spell." Nothing else made sense. I wasn't supposed to want to bed a witch. Hell, the idea should have repulsed me. I shoved those thoughts out of my brain and tried to let the scent of the game to the south of me take its place.

The storm let up, fading to a whimpering rain that lasted all night. I was bone tired, but couldn't sleep. Instead, I stared out the window and waited for the sun to rise.

When it did, I itched to head out, shift, and hunt for my break-fast. My stomach roiled in protest. I couldn't take the chance, though. Though I couldn't scent her nearly as strong anymore, the witch might still be out there. If she was as good as her word, she said she'd head back this way.

Sure enough, just past daybreak, I heard the crunch of dead branches to the southeast. I adjusted myself on the cot, letting my legs dangle over the side. When the cabin door flew open, I shielded my eyes from the sun but lay perfectly still otherwise.

She smelled like wildflowers and strong soap. Mixed with that was that dangerous something hovering just beneath. She stood in the doorway wearing a thin, loose-fitting, white cotton dress. With the sunlight at her back, the fabric turned practically transparent, showing the outline of her slender body. My eyes were drawn to the vee between her thighs. I let out a slow breath to try and steady my heart as heated blood coursed through me, pumping straight between my legs.

She slammed the door behind her and headed toward me. She had a picnic basket slung over her arm.

"I'd say you were a regular Red Riding Hood, but you don't quite look the part," I quipped.

"Neither do you, bear," she said. She took a tentative step toward me, her eyes going straight to my legs.

"Sorry to disappoint you," I said. "Whatever the hell you did to me hasn't worn off yet."

Her eyes widened with alarm, but she quickly tried to cover, licking her bottom lip and pasting on a wide smile.

"Maybe you're just a slow healer."

"Maybe *you* don't know your own strength. Now, why don't you do us both a favor and bring somebody down here who actually knows what they're doing."

"No!" She sucked in a breath then put her fake smile back in place. "No. I mean. I know what I'm doing."

She came closer and stood over the bed. Setting her picnic basket down, she smoothed her dress and folded her arms in front of her.

"So what's your plan, witch? You gonna keep me here as your hostage?"

Just a tiny tremor near the corner of her mouth betrayed her real feelings. She was scared to death. Of what I wasn't sure. I just had to figure out a way to use that to my advantage.

"I brought you breakfast. There's some fruit, lunchmeat, some chicken soup in a thermos. It's not much, but it ought to help you keep your strength up while you finish healing."

Her breasts rose and fell with her uneven breaths. Even if my bear weren't dialed into her moods, it wouldn't take much to figure out she was lying her ass off. Thank God she hadn't really struck me paralyzed because it was obvious she didn't have a damn clue how to fix it. No wonder it freaked her out so badly. Injuring a shifter like that violated the delicate truce our people shared. She knew it and I knew it. It was a far worse transgression than my questionable trespass over Salt Fork lands. It meant she needed something from me.

"Tell the truth," I said, hating myself for lying to her at the same time my more carnal nature loved watching her squirm a little. "You don't have the first clue about how to fix me."

"That's not true," she said, flapping her arms in exasperation. That little blue light sparked between her fingers and it occurred to me she didn't even realize it. She started to pace and static electricity made the hairs on my arms raise.

"Calm down," I said, using the most even tone I could. At first, her agitation had been kind of cute. I realized now it might actually be dangerous.

"I'm sorry, okay?" She turned on me. "How many times do I have to say it? You weren't supposed to be there!"

My spine started to tingle and the bear quickened inside of me.

As much as being near me seemed to send her magic haywire, she was having a similar effect on me. Except I seemed to be the only one noticing it.

"Witch, I'm telling you. Calm the fuck down."

She crossed the distance between us. "Talia. My name is Talia. It's not 'witch.'"

She raised her hand. It might just have been an innocent gesture, but I wasn't about to take the chance. Before she could react, I caught her by the wrist and pulled her down to the bed next to me. She lost her balance and landed with her full weight on top of me.

If I'd had any doubt about who or what she was, my bear answered it for me. The instant I had her close to me again with her breasts pressed against my chest, I damn near lost it. Her heart thudded against mine and the urge to kiss her made it impossible to breathe.

Mine. Mine!

That was the bear talking. Her hot breath caressed my cheek and her eyes widened. I think her own heart told her what her body craved.

"Bear, let go of me," she said, breathless. I did. She rose on unsteady legs and took a staggering step backward.

She started to pace again and wiped a hand across her face. "Shit. Okay, shit!" She turned to face me.

"Something you wanna share with the rest of the class?"

Talia flapped her arms and stopped. Talia. I liked the sound of it. Still, keeping her a little scared of me suited my plans better. So, she could only be "witch." She kept her distance this time, standing at the foot of the bed. "You're right. I don't know why you can't walk yet. I just...ugh...I need you to hang tight and give me some time to figure it out."

"Ah. So your plan is to just keep me against my will until you can un-fuck your fuckup."

Oh, God, the fury that came into her eyes ignited fresh desire inside of me. If I wasn't careful, she'd see just how *not* paralyzed I was from the waist down.

"Well, actually, yes. Except for the hostage part. I'm not holding you against your will. I'm just kind of ...well...borrowing you until I figure out how to help you."

"Ah. Well. Thanks for the clarification, except I still can't leave."

"You can leave! I mean...I wouldn't stop you. It's just...uh...things are a little complicated on my end. I'd really appreciate it if you just wouldn't go off and tell anybody about what happened."

I hooked my fingers behind my head and leaned back. God, it was fun watching her spin herself into a frenzy. Her dress twirled as she started pacing again. This was bad. Disastrous, really. Except the girl had me straight-up driven to lust-filled distraction. I could get past it, though. I'd have to. As fun as it was to watch her, she was still the best lead I had. With the way she was acting, I was pretty sure she had no personal involvement with any curse against the bears. There was nothing calculated about the herky-jerky way she wielded her power. But, that didn't mean someone close to her wasn't involved. If I kept my head and gained her trust, this could work.

"Well, witch, I'd say I'm completely at your mercy at the moment."

"You're a pain in the ass, bear." She stopped pacing. "But thank you. I mean that. And I'll figure something out. Trust me."

I watched her luscious backside as she stopped pacing and opened the door. Sunlight flooded the room again and made her dress see-through. I fisted the blankets to keep from losing control at the sight of her dark nipples through the thin fabric.

"Doesn't look like I have much of a choice, do I, witch?"

"Ugh. You're a pain in the ass, bear."

"Right, you already said that." I smirked at her. When she turned back to face me, her exasperated glower warmed my blood all over again. Damnit, I liked her on fire way too much.

"Just...stay put," she said, flapping her hands again.

I hooked my hands behind my head and leaned back. "You've pretty much made it so that's all I can do, darlin'."

She pointed her finger at me. The blue glow at the end of it made her eyes widen. She quickly curled her fist and shoved her hand behind her back. In a huff, she turned on her heel and stormed back out of the cabin.

Chapter Five

TALIA

Hot magic made my fingertips sizzle. The bear brought it out in me and the thrill of it made my heart beat faster. It shouldn't be that way. The smarter course would have been to leave him to his own devices and stay the hell away from that part of the woods until...well...forever.

Except I couldn't. He was there because of me. All it would take was one call to his bear clan and Salt Fork would be crawling with shifters of every kind. It wasn't just the bears we had a truce with. There were wolf shifters teeming along the Kentucky border just waiting for a reason to come here. Last I heard, bears and wolves weren't exactly friends either, but when it came down to it, they were all shifters and we were witches. The lines would be very clearly drawn. And once again, a Lear witch would be the root cause of disaster between shifters and witches.

I ran as fast as I could. The temperature dropped as the wind kicked up and I prayed we wouldn't get another storm so soon. It would make it more difficult for me to go back to the cabin later tonight to check on the bear. With any luck, he'd be long gone by then. I felt a small, unbidden twinge of longing at the thought of that. Almost as if I were praying he'd still be there. If he was though, it meant whatever I'd done to him might really be permanent.

God, my mother would know what to do. Even Marjorie would probably have been able to come up with a plan. They were so like each other, calm, serene. I ran hot like the Lear side. No one would ever say it to my face, but I knew Grandma Torre, my father, and even some of the other members of the coven worried I took *too* much after the Lears. My aunt hadn't been able to control the blackest parts of her magic. It had destroyed her and nearly set off a Shifter War too. But, she was gone now. Her death had been enough to quell the problem. It was up to me to make sure that stayed true.

I took the shortcut over Buck Creek. Thankfully, no one saw me emerge from the woods. I straightened my skirts and concentrated on slowing my wildly beating heart. I was already nearly half an hour late for work. As soon as I reached downtown Digby, people started coming out of the shops along Main Street. So much for not drawing attention to myself. I got friendly waves from Mr. and Mrs. Anderson who ran Digby's one and only gas station. Mrs. Anderson smiled broadly and elbowed Mr. Anderson before he said anything. I waved my hand and smiled. Mr. and Mrs. Anderson were two of the oldest witches in the coven, so of course they felt me declare. But, I knew everyone, no matter how strong their powers, knew my status. Even if the other members hadn't felt me connect to the Source, Grandma Torre had the town's biggest mouth.

I kept my head down and trudged down the street as quickly as I could. Torre Forge, the family business, took up the corner of Main and Hickory. It's tall, black smokestack is the predominant feature in Digby's sparse skyline. Today, it belched out heavy black smoke. My father ran a custom blacksmith shop that he inherited from Grandpa Torre. That's how he met my mother. She was an only child and Grandpa hired my dad as an apprentice when he was only sixteen years old. My mother had been fourteen. By the time *she* was sixteen, my father was secretly in love with her. He kept quiet until she turned eighteen.

As I approached the weathered gray siding and glass double doors, I took a steeling breath then went inside. Dad worked in the corner, his back to me, hunched over one of four massive anvils he had anchored to the floor. He didn't hear me come in as he pounded hot orange steel into what would become a Bowie knife. His powerful biceps and nimble hands punished the piece of molten metal into shape. Sometimes, I'd lose hours just marveling at the surgical precision he used to wield such powerful forces. Torre Forge makes custom knives, axes, tomahawks, and even swords on occasion. The shop had been my father's salvation after the loss of both my sister and mother just two short years apart. For a time, I felt like I'd lost him to the forge in the wake of it all. Now, we'd both made our peace and worked side by side most days in different ways.

I tucked a stray hair behind my ear and slid behind the counter. We never got a hell of a lot of walk-in traffic here besides the occasional curiosity seeker. But, the phones rang plenty. Most of our orders came to us online since I finally talked my father into letting me design a website five years ago. I'd done it when I was fourteen and he'd had me working here ever since. Business had increased tenfold since then. In another year, I'd hoped to have enough saved to finally start college and maybe even leave Digby for a while.

My back tingled. Before I could turn around, Grandma Torre came behind me and put her hands on my shoulders. She planted a big kiss on my cheek. I turned to let her wrap me in her arms and press my head against her ample bosom.

"I'm so proud of you, babydoll," she said. After she'd finished slathering me with more kisses, she let me up and held my cheeks in her hands. Her green eyes filled with tears as she smiled at me. Grandma Torre was seventy years old. She had a plump, round face and wiry gray hair that stuck out in all directions. She'd worn it in a bun for as long as I could remember.

"I told you," she said. "All you had to do was really put your mind to it. Didn't I tell you?"

"Oh, you told me. You were right."

"Do you feel all right? Sometimes the Source can make you feel a little sick the first time. It passes, though."

I nodded as she finally let go. "I'm okay. I do feel a little...uh...off kilter, though. Like it's still bigger than me."

"Oh honey, it *is*. But just relax. It doesn't take long before you figure out how to control it. It's like riding a bike."

I scrunched my nose. "So I'll never forget how to do it?"

She shook her head. "No. Like you fall the first time, but in no time, you start sailing."

I hugged her again, smiling at her mixed-up metaphor. Still, uneasiness tugged at my heart. I didn't feel the least bit of control over my powers. If only I could tell her exactly what I did. But, I couldn't risk it. The more people who knew about the bear, the worse this could get. You could get punished for so much as talking to a shifter. Although no one came out and said it, people around here had acted differently toward my family since my aunt went out and tried to interfere with the shifters. No. Until I knew what I was dealing with, it was better to limit the damage from my mistake.

More than anything, I needed to come up with a reason to get out of the shop today. Grandma and my father would be occupied here all day. It would give me ample time to run back home and get some supplies and my mother's spell diaries. She'd been one of the strongest healers the coven had seen in generations. Surely she'd written *something* I could use to try and help that bear.

Grandma stood beside me, rubbing my back. She smiled so wide I wondered if it didn't hurt her cheeks. A hollow pit formed in my stomach at the lie I kept telling. Would she still be proud of me when she found out it took a shifter to finally connect me to the Source?

"You don't look so good, honey," she said. "You look pale." Grandma put the back of her hand to my forehead. Then she grabbed my hands and turned my palms up. "You're running hot, Talia. Are you getting sparks?"

"Huh? Oh. Well, a little. Nothing I haven't been able to control." Another lie.

"Hmm. Well, that's good."

She patted my back again and I realized she'd just given me the excuse I needed, even if it meant piling a littler lie on top of the big one I kept from her. "I am kind of exhausted though. Is that normal?"

Her smile faded, but her eyes stayed kind. "It is. It doesn't last long. Do you maybe want to go and lay down in the back for a little bit? Your father's not even going to notice you're here. He's finishing up that big order. Toby's on his way in to help him."

My stomach flipped. Toby Winters was my father's apprentice. He'd taken him on at Grandma's insistence. The Winters family was one of the oldest in the coven. He'd been my sister's age and years ago, he'd had a crush on her. I remember him following Marjorie around like a puppy. It creeped me out and even at eight years old, I'd told her she should tell him to get lost. But, Marjorie could never be that mean. Now, Toby seemed to be my problem.

"You know, Grandma, I really would like to get some rest. Do you think it would be okay if I just went home until after lunch? I've been out at the cabin for days. It's not just the declaration that's got me cooked. I need a warm shower and a hot meal."

Grandma's mouth dropped open. "You mean to say you came straight from the woods? Oh, for heaven's sake, babydoll. You march right on home now. I'll handle things with your dad. I'll head over to check on you in a couple of hours. I've got a stew on for dinner and I need to add some garlic and basil."

"I can do that," I said, sliding off my stool. I leaned in and kissed her on the forehead. I was only five foot two, but flat-footed I towered over Grandma Torre. She gave me a hug and swatted my backside as I slipped around the counter and headed for the door.

God, I hated deceiving her. But, for now, there was no other way. I set a brisk pace as I crossed the street and headed the six blocks to the Purple House. The Purple House had been in the Lear family for over one hundred and fifty years. It was a huge, three-story Victorian home with a wrap-around porch, high dormer windows, a multicolored slate roof and one great spire in the front corner reaching to the sky. The house had been painted garish violet for as long as anyone could remember. I reached the edge of our picket fence when a shadow loomed in front of me.

"Talia!" Toby's deep voice shook through me. He seemed to come from nowhere. I turned, shielding my eyes from the sun as he jogged across the street.

"Toby," I said, trying to keep my voice light. Before I could stop him, Toby grabbed me into a hug and twirled me off my feet. He'd always been too familiar, but this time, my skin seemed to burn where he touched me. I pushed back and he let me go, dropping me hard.

"What's wrong with you?" he said. Toby grabbed my upper arm and turned me back to face him. He had thick, sandy-blond hair that stuck out in peaks in the front. A jagged scar cut through his left eyebrow from when he'd fallen off his bike and hit the curb when he ten years old. It had happened right in front of our house. He was tall. In fact, until I'd met the bear, Toby Winters had been the tallest boy I'd ever known at six foot two.

"I'm just feeling a little under the weather," I said, forcing a smile. "I'm going to go in and rest for a bit. Then I'm heading back to the shop. Why aren't you there now? My father's going to need your help more than ever today."

Toby's face fell. He hadn't loosened his grip on my arm. He pulled me toward him just a little and it took everything in me not to jerk away. I'd always been somewhat cold to Toby, not wanting him to ever misinterpret my intentions. He looked at me as the next best thing after Marjorie. I knew even my father and Grandma Torre thought we'd make a good match. For my father's part, I think he liked the story of it more than anything else. History repeating itself. Except Toby Winters was nothing like my father and I was nothing like my mother. No one had forced the issue, though. Now, something powerful rose up inside of me. I felt the energy crackling just below the surface. I took a steeling breath, trying to stave off the witchfire my fingers wanted to make.

"I felt you, you know. We all did. You're dialed in hard to the Source now. It surprised me. How'd you finally do it?"

"Do what, Toby?"

He gave me a half-smile. "You know, a lot of us were starting to think maybe you were a dud."

This time, I finally did tear myself out of his grip. I don't know what he saw in my eyes, but it was enough to make Toby's narrow in near-menace. He took a step toward me.

"I'm really not in the mood for this right now, okay? I'm wiped out. I'm heading inside to rest. I'll see you later."

"Talia, something's different about you. What is it?" My heart raced. Toby cocked his head to the side and sniffed the air. He wrinkled his nose in disgust.

"I've been out in the woods for three days, okay? I need a shower. But thanks for pointing it out."

Toby let out a snort. "It's not that, Talia. Your magic smells...uh...wrong. What the hell did you do out there?"

"Nothing! And it's none of your business anyway. It's personal. You of all people should know that. Look, the whole town knows I've declared. That's it. End of story. Everyone should be happy I'm not the lone Lear lemon. Now if you'll just let me get inside, I'd really appreciate it. It's been a long, long few days."

Toby crossed his arms in front of him and shifted his weight away from me, but the scowl didn't leave his face. Anger flared inside of me. He had no right to judge me. He had no right to even ask me any of this.

"Fine," he said. "I'll see you at the shop later. For the love of God, take that shower. Take three of them. You smell awful."

I resisted the urge to flip Toby off. Instead, I gave him the fakest smile I could muster and headed through the gate into the house. I couldn't help myself. The minute I shut the front door, I sniffed under my arm. What the hell was he talking about?

Fear speared through me as I guessed. Was it possible Toby could smell the bear? No. It couldn't be. Grandma Lear would have been able to tell in a heartbeat. Still, Toby's accusing eyes unsettled me. The last thing I needed was to rouse his suspicions about anything that happened out in those woods yesterday. I locked the door behind me and pressed the back of my head against the solid oak.

I let out a hard breath. Grandma Torre would be back in a little more than an hour. It wouldn't give me much time. She kept my mother's diaries in her bedroom beneath her four-poster bed. If she caught me looking there, she probably wouldn't care. But, I just didn't want to be in a position to lie to her yet again.

I took the winding stairs two at a time. I stopped just outside Marjorie's bedroom just like I always did. My father kept it just as she'd left it, with her canopy princess bed and pink wallpaper. My sister collected stuffed horses and said she had plans to buy a horse farm out past Freedom Road when she was old enough to afford it. She would have. Marjorie always did everything she set her mind to, until the day she couldn't anymore.

Letting my fingers trail along the six-paneled door, I made my way to Grandma's bedroom at the end of the hall. She had an assortment of half-finished embroidery projects all over the tops of her dresser and slung over one corner of her bed. I carefully pushed them aside and leaned down. I lifted her eyelet dust ruffle and pulled out the three green leather-bound books with the broken locks and gold embossed lettering. Grandma had cut those locks the day after my mother died. That was two years after we lost Marjorie. As good a healer as she was, she couldn't fight the form of cancer that ravaged her body so quickly. Everyone said the trauma of losing the both of them is what kept me from being able to declare for so long. Now, I wondered what they would say.

Clutching the diaries to my chest, I replaced the dust ruffle and left my grandma's bedroom. I went up the flight of stairs next to Grandma's door and into my attic bedroom. I'd moved up here after my eighteenth birthday. We'd converted it into a small apartment with a living area and TV in one corner, a small bathroom in the other, and my bed facing the northeast dormer window. It was private and quiet up here. Grandma couldn't manage the second flight of stairs and my father didn't like going past Marjorie's room for anything.

I set the small volumes on the bed and opened the first one. My mother's neat, slanted cursive covered each page. I'd read each of these hundreds of times to the point I almost knew them by heart. She wrote down recipes, random thoughts, various herb combinations she'd found useful, and a dozen or more healing spells. She hadn't invented these spells. That art was lost even to a witch as powerful as my mother had been. But, she'd written notes in the margins, tweaking them here and there to produce better results. There was one for fevers, another for pain. Once, she'd found a bird with broken wing and helped it mend. That's the one I looked for. Although a full-grown bear shifter was entirely different matter, I figured that was the closest I could come.

I found the spell in the second book on the last page. The words were simple and it called for fire magic. That surprised me. I would have guessed earth magic. That was my mother's specialty, just like it was for almost *all* the Torres, Grandma included. Lears were fire mages. It's one of the reasons my father was such a gifted bladesmith. Me? Well, it seemed the fire had finally called me. The warmth flooding through my fingertips whenever the bear got close to me gave me hope that I could be onto something with this spell.

I slipped the spellbook into my canvas backpack. I just had to hope the weather cooperated. If another storm came, it would be too risky to head back out to the cabin to try the spell. I could barely control the magic I *had* tapped into. Whipping up a fire spell in the middle of a lightning storm might kill us both.

Now, there was nothing to do but wait. I decided to leave a note for Dad and Grandma. Another lie, but really it was more just a bending of the truth. I'd tell them I wanted more practice with the Source. It was normal for a newly declared witch to spend time alone among the elements. In fact, it's probably what both of them would have suggested anyway. Still, that guilty hollow space formed in my gut. With any luck, the spell would work and I could send the bear back to his people with no one the wiser. I sure as hell didn't think he'd have the urge to go blabbing that a five foot two, hundred and ten-pound witch got the best of him.

When Grandma came home to check on the stew at lunchtime, I stayed in my attic apartment. She called up once, but I knew she thought I was sleeping. When she left to go back to the shop, I took my shower, changed into a clean dress, laced up my hiking boots, and lit out for the woods. I put a generous serving of Grandma's stew in a plastic container along with a half-gallon of milk in my backpack and headed back out toward Freedom Road. With any luck, I'd get to the cabin just before sunset.

The skies stayed mercifully clear as I veered off the main trail and moved deeper into the woods. Sizzling energy coursed through me with each step I took. I could sense the bear. God, how had I missed him the first time? His signature cut a wide, heated swath all around me. It made my heart beat faster and my limbs tingle. I wondered if he could sense me just as easily. The idea of it made me freeze where I stood. So stupid of me not to think of it. If Hogwarts were an actual thing, Shifter Cloaking 101 would have been a Freshman Year course. My grandmother had told me how to do it all my life, but I'd never been quite able to pull it off. Now, with the energy from the Source flowing through my veins as naturally as blood, I closed my eyes and concentrated on slowing my breathing. I let the heat flooding my body subside, until I felt a cool breeze at my back. When I opened my eyes, just the faintest blue glow emanated from my fingertips.

I kept walking, feeling stronger and more confident now that I knew I could approach the cabin without him sensing me so easily. The last glint of sunlight guided my path as I cut across Buck Creek and covered the final two hundred yards. The cabin was straight ahead. It looked quiet and abandoned. That should have made me relieved, but a sharp pang of desperation went through me. It nearly made me drop my shielding spell. I got a hold of myself and changed direction, heading for the cabin toward the back of it.

A branch snapped to my right. Dropping low, I hid behind a bush. I waited. It was then I noticed the door of the cabin stood wide open. I hadn't left it like that. I was sure of it. Heat zinged along my spine. I let the backpack slide off my shoulder. Movement behind me made the hair along my arms stand on end. A shadow darkened the patch of ground in front of me. I waited for my moment, then sprang up and turned.

Blue light danced from my fingertips as the bear came into view. He was huge and glorious, the largest grizzly I'd ever seen. He stood on his hind legs and sniffed the air. He came down on his massive front paws, making the ground vibrate from the impact. He couldn't see me. He sensed something different, but he damn well couldn't see me!

He swung his great, domed head low and sniffed again, taking in great gulps of air. He let out a short chuff, then stretched his paws forward, arching his back. His thick, brown fur rippled and he lifted his head up. His bones crunched and his back twisted to an impossible angle as muscles and sinew remade themselves.

My heart pumped so loud I thought surely he could hear it. Energy flooded through me at the proximity to such powerful magic. I ached to feel his skin beneath my fingertips and draw from his strength. His back finally straightened and his claws receded, long fingers taking their place. His skin stretched and the bones of his face grew. Black eyes became dark brown, lit with keen intelligence. He rose on strong, supple legs. The muscles of his calves and thighs flexed as he righted himself. My eyes traveled up and up. He turned toward me, still unaware that I was there. I saw him in his full, naked glory. His heavy cock swung between his legs and the heat of desire flared through me.

He was beautiful, powerful, and full of magic that should have terrified me. Instead, I was drawn to it. So much so that I took a step toward him without thinking. A twig snapped beneath my foot. He flinched and turned in the direction of the sound. I froze, but it was too late. He couldn't see me, but now he knew I was there. His eyes flashed dark as he came toward me. Fire magic flooded my senses as my nature tried to repel his even as my desire heated my core.

"Witch," he said, his voice full of the same heat that filled me.

He took one more step toward me as blue fire shot from my fingertips. This time, he was ready for it and dodged to the side. He was quicker than I was. He recovered and lunged for me before I could bring my hands up a second time. He pinned me to the ground, holding my wrists above my head, and he covered me with the full length of his body.

Chapter Six

RAFE

I braced myself above her. She wriggled beneath me; her body gave off pure, molten magic. That snapping blue light poured from her fingertips. It went into me where I held her wrists above her head, even though she couldn't aim it. The hairs on my arms singed and warmth flooded my nerve endings. God, it was pleasure and pain all rolled into one. The bear hovered just below the surface. She called to it even though she couldn't know what she was doing. Her fierce eyes stared into mine, challenging me. Her breasts trembled beneath the thin cotton of her dress as she gasped for air.

I let go of her wrists and planted my palms on either side of her, keeping my body above hers, no more than an inch separating us. As her breath mixed with mine, I felt my cells shifting, realigning, like metal filings pulled to a magnet. A groan escaped my lips and her eyelids hooded. She brought her hands up. It was a subtle gesture, but instead of pushing me away, she played her fingers along my bare shoulders. That kinetic energy flowed from her and directly into me. My bear simmered, wanting her. Her magic was white heat and power. I felt it as she trailed her fingers along my arms.

I stayed stock still, afraid if I moved even a little, I wouldn't be able to keep the bear contained. Her touch set off a fire inside of me. She seemed to feed off it. We fed off each other, her power against mine. It was primal lust and wonder. It was nothing I'd ever felt before.

Then, she moved. Her eyelids fluttered and she craned her neck upward. I kept my arms steady, caging her between them. She moved her hands from my arms and touched my face.

"Bear," she gasped. She touched her lips to mine.

She had no idea what she was doing. Her body just responded to the overpowering need that slammed through her just as it did me. *Anam Cara.* I was told it would feel like this. A pull stronger than any instinct I'd ever felt.

My vision went dark and my body trembled. Her quick little tongue darted out and I couldn't stay still a second longer. A growl escaped me and I slid my arm around her. I rolled, bringing her on top of me as I kissed her back. She was dark and sweet all at once. The power from her fingertips held been just a hint of the greater magic locked inside of her. My cock throbbed and grew rock hard. A few more seconds of this and I wasn't sure I could hold myself back. I wasn't sure she could either. We devoured each other with heated lips and probing tongues. More. I wanted more. I saw swirling lightning in my mind's eye as she pressed her body against mine.

Finally, she pulled back, gasping for air. She kept my face between her palms. Her swollen bottom lip trembled.

"Bear," she whispered again. "What are you?" It hadn't hit her yet.

She hadn't processed what she'd just done or what it could mean. She was still running on pure adrenaline and instinct.

Except, I knew it was the wrong question. I couldn't bring myself to tell her that. Not yet. Not until I could make more sense of it myself. Because the real question was, what was she?

I put my hands up, palms out in a non-threatening gesture. Though she'd initiated the kiss, that crackling energy still poured from her. I didn't know how witches worked, but she clearly didn't seem to have full command of her power. She reminded me very much of a young shifter, still struggling to harness his shift. Maybe witches worked the same way. Whatever the answer was, I didn't want to be on the receiving end of another lightning blast she didn't intend.

Talia blinked hard and came back into herself. She gathered her skirts and rolled off of me. Drawing her knees up, she wrapped her arms around herself and stared at me. Her eyes traveled downward and I realized she was getting a full view of the exact effect she had on me. Stark naked after my shift, my cock was rigid. I sat up and got my legs beneath me. Talia's eyes stayed riveted to my dick and there was no mistaking the desire behind them. I cleared my throat and walked two yards away where I'd left my jeans in a heap. I pulled them on and ran a hand through my hair as I turned back to her.

"Who are you?" she asked. "I mean, what's your name?"

I couldn't help it. The question made me laugh. It seemed so simple and sort of beside the point at the moment. But, maybe it was progress. Lust was one thing; what I really needed from her was trust.

"Rafe," I said. "I'm the McCormack Alpha." She cocked her head to the side and a line of confusion formed between her brows. Of course, my clan name wouldn't mean a whole lot to a witch. She was starting to grow skittish. Turmoil clouded her eyes as she tried to make sense of what had just happened. I knew full well what it was, but I sensed she wasn't ready to hear it. Hell, I wasn't sure I was ready for it either. But the thrumming desire between my legs would undo me one way or the other. I did my level best to push all lustful urges out of my head and focus on what had brought me here in the first place. I needed her help. My men were dying. No matter what I felt for her, clan business came first.

I held out a hand to her. She bit her bottom lip. A slow blush crept into her cheeks that sent fresh heat racing through me. But, she took my hand and stood.

"You're better," she said, picking leaves from her dress.

"Compared to what?"

"Compared to yesterday. You can walk."

"Let's go inside," I said. "I don't like the looks of the eastern sky and you seem to have a knack for drawing lightning down on our heads. We need to talk."

She could have left. It would have been her wisest course. But, I knew she wouldn't. Whatever the hell it was between us, it had her just as unsettled as it did me. She couldn't turn away from it any more than I could. So, she gathered her backpack off the ground where she'd dropped it and followed me inside.

I was too keyed up to sit. I ended up pacing the floor while Talia took a seat on the cot. She pulled a faded green book out of her backpack then drew her legs up again and sat hugging them while I covered the floor.

"How do you feel?" she finally said. "I mean, your legs. You can walk. You can shift. There's nothing else wrong with you, is there? I didn't do any permanent damage?"

I stopped pacing. "So far so good. But what were you planning to do if I hadn't got better?" I didn't like lying to her about how seriously she'd hurt me. If I told her the truth now, it might shatter whatever thin layer of trust we had. I wished I hadn't been so careless as to let her find me like that outside. She'd done something, though, a spell maybe. It's the only thing that could have kept me from sensing her. The fact that she'd figured out how to control her magic so quickly unsettled me at the same time it made a flare of pride run through me. She was something special. I'd known it from the second I laid eyes on her.

She reached out and placed a flat palm on the green book beside her. "There was a spell I wanted to try."

I went to her. My heart thundered inside my chest. A spell. Another fucking spell. I had just enough of my father in me to recoil in disgust. Shielding herself was one thing; letting her voluntarily cast a spell on me or my kind set my nerves on edge.

"What kind of spell?"

Talia pursed her lips. I could tell she was at war with herself about telling me any more. She seemed to struggle with the same mistrust I had. I backed off, putting distance between us; I sat down on the hearth and worked my thumb into the opposite palm as I waited for her to make up her mind.

"It's a healing spell. My mother used it a long time ago. I'm not even sure I can work it. I'm not...I don't think I have the kind of magic she did."

"There's more than one kind?"

Talia rolled her eyes. "I didn't figure a bear would understand." My question offended her and I didn't know why. She must have read something on my face because she dropped her indignation and spread her hands out as she tried to explain.

"There's not just one kind of shifter, right? I mean, you're not the same as a werewolf, are you?"

An involuntary noise ripped from my throat. I coughed to cover it, realizing my defensive reaction was just about the same as she'd just given me. There was so much we didn't understand about each other.

"I didn't know that. I didn't know witches had different magics. I didn't mean to offend you."

She raised a brow and nodded, accepting my attempt at an apology. "Fair enough. My mother was an earth mage. She drew most of her power from other living things. They're the best healers. She had a spell I saw her use to fix a bird's wing once. I was very little and it had flown into a window."

I rubbed my palm on my jeans. "What do you mean she drew her power from other living things. You mean she *took* from them? As in, she drained them to serve her own ends?"

Talia's eyes flashed dark. "Bear, maybe you should just listen. I'm trying very hard to give you the benefit of the doubt about stuff you don't understand."

Her fury called to mine. It took great effort not to grab her and accuse her of what was happening to my people on the ridge. Is that what this was? Was there some filthy earth witch drawing life from us to serve her own needs?

"So explain it, witch. I'm still listening."

"Earth mages don't *take* from other living things. It's not stealing. Every living thing on the planet, including *you*, draws power from the earth. It's constant. It doesn't go away. It's a circle. I'm surprised you don't know more about the very force that allows you to *be*."

"So enlighten me," I said. I leaned back against the stone hearth and crossed my ankle over the opposite knee. God, even when she was pissed at me, I couldn't stop thinking about how much I wanted to kiss her again.

"Your magic is earth-based too. That's all I'm saying. When you shift into your bear, are you taking something from other beings? No. Of course not. It's just how you...work. When you die, you become part of the earth again. Renewal, rebirth, life, death. It's all the same thing."

I flipped my hand, conceding her point. "Fine. I get it. But, what about you? What kind of witch are you?"

I thought it was an innocent enough question, but the color drained from Talia's face and tension went into her shoulders. My instinct told me to go to her, to comfort her. I didn't want to see her in distress of any kind. I curled my fists at my side and willed myself still.

"I'm still sort of trying to figure that out."

I couldn't help it. Her answer made me laugh. "You think? Because my charbroiled spine begs to differ."

She puffed out her cheeks and blew out an exasperated breath. God, I loved how her eyes flashed fire when she was pissed at me, which was pretty much all the time.

I flattened my hands on the hearth. "Look. I'm sorry. I didn't mean anything by that. As much as your kind would probably like to believe otherwise, I'm not as dumb as I look. You said your mother was an earth mage. So, I'm guessing there are such things as wind mages, water mages...and in your case fire mages."

I wanted to go to her. Her crestfallen expression tugged at my heart. She didn't have to explain any more. I didn't need to understand every facet of what a witch was. I knew enough. She reminded me of me when I first began to understand the beast I carried within me. It had been so hard to control. All shifters spend years learning how to understand the power we carry. It's such a simple thing, really. But, when you're new at it, it can overwhelm you and rip you apart. It takes practice and maturity to understand that power isn't something you should ever try to control. You just let it be part of you. I could see Talia's fear written plainly in her eyes, and it spoke to me. I wanted to tell her. But, I knew she'd never accept the word of a shifter. Just like me, she'd been raised to fear and distrust my kind.

"I should go," she said. She rose and shoved her little green book in her backpack. "We're even now. You're healed. You don't need me."

She moved quickly, brushing past me; she headed for the door. Without making a conscious choice to do it, I circled my hand around her wrist and stopped her. That same powerful heat traveled from me to her and back again.

"Are you sure *you* don't need *me*?"

She sucked in a breath and her eyelids fluttered. The truth was inside of her and it scared her. I wanted nothing more than to take that fear away and quiet her doubts with a kiss. But, I had doubts of my own. I had men depending on me. I believed now more than ever that my journey to Salt Fork had been part of an unfolding fate. Talia was my fate. I softened my grip and my expression.

"Just wait," I said. "You can't leave yet, witch."

"Bear, let go of me. We don't have anything left to talk about." Her skin heated. I knew in another second she'd fill with that blue fire. I'd done the one thing I wanted to avoid. I had her scared. So, I tried another tact...the truth.

"What if I told you I need you?"

"For what? Your legs work. You can shift. You shouldn't be here. If another member of the coven figures out you're out here, it's going to be bad for you. You need to go back to wherever it is you came from."

I took a step back, towering over her. I slid my hand up her arm and caressed her cheek. Talia's lips parted and she tilted her face toward mine. The urge to kiss her poured through me as hard as I knew it did through her.

"At a certain point, we're going to have to talk about that," I said, running my thumb along her bottom lip. Her cheeks flushed. I could *feel* the heat pouring through her, settling low in her belly. God. I ached for her. With every fiber of my being I knew if I touched her sex, I'd find her wet for me.

Talia found the strength to pull away. She took a faltering step back; her breasts heaved as she tried to catch her breath. Oh, yes, her desire nearly drove her senseless.

"I don't...it's just...I'm not used to being around shifters. It isn't natural."

I couldn't help it, that got a laugh out of me. I shouldn't worry so much about lying to her; she was doing enough of it to herself. Unusual? Yes, but what I felt when she was near me was the most natural thing in the world.

"Your mother's spell," I said, trying to steer her attention to something easier for her to grapple. "Do you think it could work to heal a shifter?"

She squared her shoulders and turned toward me. "But, you're not sick."

I shook my head. "No. But a friend of mine is. He's very sick and nothing we've tried seems to be helping."

Talia's eyes widened and she looked toward the door as if she were scared someone might burst through it.

"I can't help you," she said quickly. "I've spent too much time with you already."

"Witch," I said, softening my voice. "You owe me."

"For what?"

"For zapping me and leaving me paralyzed for two days." I hated lying to her, but the guilty look in her eyes told me this might work. "You broke the truce. Bears are connected, you know. I'm a Clan Alpha. My crew knows something happened." Another white lie, but Talia's mouth formed a tight 'o' and I knew I had her.

"I told you, I'm not even sure I can work that spell."

"But, you thought it was worth a try on me. You were willing to take the risk. I'm just asking you to take it."

"Where's your friend?" Talia went to the window. She put her hands on her hips and whirled back to face me. "There's just you. I'd have sensed another bear."

"He's not here. He's back home. I want to take you to him."

"What? Are you out of your mind? You want me to march into shifter country with you. No way. No fucking way."

I went to her. My vision darkened and I knew my bear eyes glinted. God, I could barely contain myself around this girl. I was right that she didn't fully understand the magic inside of her. But, it was far more than whether she drew her power from earth or fire. As if to prove it to myself again, I put a hand on her upper arm. My heart thundered inside of me and Talia's eyes snapped wide. Oh, yes, she had magic inside of her she didn't understand. It wasn't just witch magic. She *was* an Anam Cara. Had I any doubts, she quashed those when her body answered mine with powerful desire.

This woman. This witch. She was born to be a bear's mate. As far as I knew, no witch ever had before. But, there was no denying it. A furious pulse beat in her temple as her senses sharpened at my touch. Even now, the fire inside of her burned brighter. She drew strength from it. She drew strength from *me*.

Talia was *my* mate. I knew it with absolute clarity as I looked into her eyes.

"I need you," I said. "Like it or not, you need me too. When you quit trying to fight it, you'll understand exactly why."

Talia jerked her arm out of my grip and backed away. "No. You're out of your damn bear mind."

I hadn't yet given voice to what I knew about her. I didn't have to. Talia began to understand even as her mind and generations of things she'd been taught railed against it. Mine did too, but I knew what my body felt. Talia was mine. I was hers.

The trouble was, I knew it might also destroy us both.

Chapter Seven

TALIA

The door hit me in the ass as I tried to leave. I couldn't breathe. I couldn't think. It had to be someone else's magic that drew me to the bear. Nothing else made sense. And yet, as I stood there staring him down, every instinct inside of me tried to pull me to him. The lingering touch of his kiss consumed my thoughts. I wanted more of it. I wanted to taste him. I wanted to drown in him and give in to the carnal thoughts that threatened to drive me mad.

A spell. It had to be. There was no other rational explanation for what I felt when I was near him. He was a *bear!* A savage killer. I knew my history. I'd heard the stories. A thousand years ago his kind had tried to destroy mine. I could *never* forget who and what he was. If it wasn't a spell making my instincts go haywire, it had to be the dumb luck of having him near me when I finally tapped into the Source. Maybe it was messing with my brain.

He looked at me with questioning eyes as I fumbled for the door-knob. I should run. I should fling whatever power I had in me straight into his chest and never look back. How dare he trespass into witch lands and ask for *our* help?

"I can't help you," I said. "I can't even be around you. Can't you see that?"

God, he was so calm. He looked at me with an infuriating smirk. Dark knowledge played behind his eyes. He seemed to enjoy the fact that being near him unsettled me as much as it did. It should have unsettled *him*. Why the hell didn't it? How the hell had I let myself get swept up in lust for...a bear?

"Witch," he said. Then, he spread his hands out, showing me his palms. "Talia. Look, this is kind of hard for me too. I never thought I'd be in the position to beg for help from a witch, but that's what I'm doing."

"Why?"

Rafe's face fell. He was hiding something from me. Though I'd only known him for a couple of days, I believed it in my soul. The thing was, I *wanted* to trust him. As much as I wanted to convince myself of it, part of me knew it wasn't just some short-circuited, misplaced lust. There was something else drawing me to him. I knew the sensible thing to do was run as far away from here as I could. And yet, guilt bound me to him as strong as any unseen magic at work here.

"I'm trying to figure out a way to trust you." It was the most honest thing either of us had said to each other. "The problem is, I really don't have any other choice. So, I'm going to tell you some things and I need you to listen with as open a mind as you can."

My fingers trembled as I held onto the doorknob. The air in the room seemed to change. It became charged with the words Rafe held onto. I knew in my soul I would be able to mark my life as before and after from this moment forward. Stay or go. This side of the door held darkness, mystery, and the impossible pull I felt toward this bear. The other side of the door was my world and everything I'd ever been taught to believe. The easy choice was to open it and run back through the woods I'd known since I was a baby. My father was on the other side of this door. My people. But, this side of the door held a familiar magic that I couldn't deny.

I don't remember making a conscious choice, but before I knew it, I let go of the doorknob. I took a hesitant step forward, gathered my skirt, and slowly sat down on the hearth. Rafe's dark eyes widened. He towered over me, crossing his arms in front of him; the hard-cut muscles of his biceps rippled as he searched for what to say to me. Finally, he sank slowly onto the cot and folded his hands in front of him as he faced me.

"You know, I figured you'd bolt," he said. "I had this speech prepared in my mind, but now that you're listening, I'm not really sure where to start."

I opened my mouth to say something, then realized I was having the exact same problem. I snapped my teeth shut. Taking a deep breath, I tried again. "Start with what happened out there. You kissed me."

He reared his head back and smiled. "Witch, you kissed *me*."

Anger flared behind my chest. I blinked hard, then realized he was right. I *had* kissed him. "Well, you sure as hell didn't do much to stop me."

"Magic," he said. "You've got a different kind inside of you than you think."

I rubbed my hands over the tops of my thighs. Fear prickled along my spine. I didn't want to hear this. I hated the set of his jaw. He seemed so sure of himself. So sure that he knew something about me that I didn't.

"Don't lecture me about my magic. You can't know more about it than I do."

He smiled and it cut through me, making that familiar warmth overload my senses. I *had* to shake it off and think with reason, not emotion.

"You ever heard the term *Anam Cara?*" he said.

I squinted at him. I rolled the word over in my head. "It's Celtic. *Soul...friend?* I don't know. I'm a little better with Latin."

Rafe's smile melted me. It was filled with a tenderness I didn't expect. He reached for me. My body went rigid as he gathered my hands into his lap and held them there. "I suppose that's close enough if we're being literal. But, I'm not. An *Anam Cara* is something important to my people. To bear shifters only. It sort of means soulmate. But, more accurately, a bear's mate. One that's fated. It's a human magic, though. I've never heard of a witch that possessed it. An *Anam Cara* is someone who's destined to mate with a bear. A *specific* bear. Through their union, new bear shifters are born."

"You're saying *I'm* one?" I recoiled, but Rafe's steadfast expression and light grip on my hands kept me still.

"Yes." Rafe answered so plainly and with such finality, that single word seemed to take physical shape and smack me dead center in the chest.

"You think I'm a bear's mate?" I tried to stand, but Rafe wouldn't let go of me.

"I know you are. And you know it too. You've known it since the second you touched me."

"No. You're out of your mind. It's a trick. A spell. Someone else is doing this."

Rafe kept my eyes. Later, I might be able to appreciate the earnest look he gave me. Pain flashed across his face, and if I had been better able to control the emotions flooding through me, I might have been sensitive to it. As it was, I felt like the earth had opened up and swallowed me. The answer was literally staring me in the face. *Anam Cara*. A bear's mate. God, even as my mind railed against it, my body...my *soul*...seemed to cry out for his. *Yes! Yes!*

"No!" I finally ripped my hands out of his and rose. I whirled away from him and headed for the door. Again, my fingers trembled as I reached for it. Again, I knew the space separating the two halves of my life was the width of that threshold.

"Talia, look at me."

I closed my eyes as my fingers hovered over the doorknob. I sucked in a hard breath, straightened my back, and turned to face him again. "Do you know what you've done? Because, I do. Maybe they don't teach you about the things shifters have done to witches. You've destroyed us."

"You're still here," he said. "So am I. And do you think witches are blameless? Do you want to know what *I* was raised knowing?" Rafe stood. He was so very tall. He filled my field of vision, blocking out the light behind him and everything else in the room. Even as my mind railed against it, my body called to his. I wanted to feel his hands all over me. I wanted to lose myself in his touch.

"I can't even tell you the worst of it," I said. "There's a blood oath. I could be punished for even talking to you, let alone..."

"Then let me tell *you* the worst of it. Witches are the reason there might not be any shifters left in a few generations. Did you know that? I said *Anam Cara* can produce new bear shifters, but generally only male ones. Do you know what I'm risking by even talking about that with you? Genocide. That's what witches have done to shifters. I can probably count on one hand the number of female bear shifters that still exist in the world. Witches did that. Your spells. Circean spells. That's what you are, aren't you? And your people are trying to do it again."

My mouth fell open. Rage bubbled up inside of me. "You know nothing. More than a thousand years ago your kind massacred our elders. You burned down our libraries. You have no idea what we lost." My lips trembled with the secret. I couldn't admit it to him. I'd told him too much already. But, in those fires, we lost our oldest grimoires. With them, we lost so much of our language. We lost the ability to cast new spells. Shifters did that. *Rafe's* kind did that. How could he stand there and try to make me believe I had shifter magic inside of me?

He tore a hand through his hair and turned his back to me. "Ludicrous. This is ludicrous. You really think the two of us are going to solve this problem by talking about it? I'm not making apologies or excuses for things that happened a thousand years before either of us were born. I'm not asking you to either. All I know is what's staring me in the face and making my heart damn near explode inside of my chest. Dammit, Talia. You know what you are. You can feel it. Are you going to stand there, two feet away from me and tell me you don't want what I do, even though I know you also want to rip my damn face off?"

He took my hand, splayed my fingers wide, and smashed it against his chest just over his heart. It *did* feel like it might explode right out of him. His pulse pounded beneath my fingertips. My own flared to match it. I felt his desire right along with my own. It singed me from the inside out, making my knees weak and my vision cloud. Oh, God. I *wanted* him. I *belonged* with him. What if he was right about everything?

I meant to tear my hand away. I had a dozen insults to hurl as I would have turned and stormed out the door. But, as Rafe's pulse beat in time with mine, the call of my magic, wherever it came from, was far too strong to fight. Before I knew what I was doing, I went up on my tiptoes, slid my other hand along his arm, and rested it on his shoulder. His eyes went black as his own magic struggled to take physical form. The bear. His heat. And mine.

His arms went around my waist. He pulled me off my feet and when his lips found mine, lightning crackled all around us. I'd brought the storm inside. I saw Rafe through a blue haze. His kiss. His touch. His scent. It was all over me, making my sex throb, aching to be filled. By him. Oh, God. I wanted him inside of me. I'd never felt anything like it. I couldn't tell him what I was. He already knew. *Anam Cara,* maybe. But beyond that, I was a virgin. Until that very moment, I hadn't fully understood why. It was this. Him. Nothing else would have ever satisfied.

His hands were everywhere. I tore at his shirt, wanting desperately to feel his bare skin against mine. He felt the same pull. With skillful fingers, he unbuttoned the front of my dress and found my stiff nipples. I groaned with pleasure as he worked them into hard peaks. I threw my head back and carved my hands through his hair as his lips found their way to my breasts. He pulled and sucked. Heat throbbed between my legs and he soon had me soaked.

It was everything. It was too much. Light and flame. Fire and ash. How could I have ever doubted where this power came from? The air sizzled as my magic poured out of me. It was so hot, so good. Blue lightning snaked around us, wrapping and binding us together.

"Talia," he whispered my name. "Witch.'"

I would have answered him. I meant to beg him for the release my body so desperately craved. But Rafe's eyes rolled back. He faltered and his grip loosened. I slid down the length of him until my feet touched the floor.

"Bear?" I gasped. He didn't look right. His claws came out but his color went gray. He reached for me, keeling over like a great oak tree. Somehow, I had the strength to catch him and guide him gently to the floor.

"What is it?"

"What did you do to me?" he croaked.

"What? I didn't. Nothing." But that wasn't true. A war raged inside of me. At the same time I wanted nothing more than to give myself to him, old ancient magics rebelled against it.

He was burning up. His shirt was half off and I carefully slid his arms out of it. Rafe rolled to the side away from me. As the blue light from my fingertips receded, his color seemed to come back. But, his shocked expression tore at me.

"Rafe? Can you hear me?"

Coughing, he nodded. "Yeah."

"I wasn't trying to hurt you."

Color came back into his cheeks at the same time his eyes grew large with terror. He sat up and pulled at his shoulder, straining to see what I did. His posture went slack and he buried his face in his hands.

"I know," he said. "Talia, there's so much more I need to say to you. But, I've got to get back to the ridge."

God. I didn't want him to go.

"What I need is to tell you why I really came here," he said.

"What are you talking about?"

"There's a sickness running through the clans at Wild Ridge. It's based in witchcraft. A spell of some kind. It's killing us. I was sent down here to find a cure. And now, I'm asking you to help me."

I shook my head and scrambled backward. I didn't like the look in his eyes. He seemed desperate and for the first time, truly afraid. "No way. I told you, I'm under an oath not to even *talk* to you. We wouldn't do this. It has to be something else."

He took a step toward me but froze when his phone rang in his back pocket. He held up a finger and put the phone to his ear.

"Yes," he said. His eyes darted as he listened to the caller on the other end. His expression hardened and he pursed his lips together. Letting out a great sigh, he slowly closed his eyes and nodded.

"I'll be there in a few hours. No! Just keep him still and quiet until I get there."

He clicked off the phone and slid it back into his jeans pocket. His eyes had changed in the last few seconds, going dark and distant. He clenched his jaw hard, held his hand out as if he were going to pull me to him, then thought better of it and let his fist fall to his side.

"I have to go."

"What is it?" My heart pounded double time. He was leaving. It was the thing I'd hoped for for days; now that he was really planning to leave, a desperate fear snaked its way up my spine.

"We aren't...finished."

He swallowed hard and met my eyes. "No, we aren't. Not by a

long shot. I need you to think about what I said and see if you can find it in your heart to trust me. I can't tell you everything yet, but if you can't help me, well...then we're already dead."

My throat went dry. Rafe didn't wait for an answer from me. He put a light hand on my shoulder, then stepped around me and went out the door.

Chapter Eight

RAFE

Bo's words rang in my head as I walked out of the cabin. It tore something inside of me to leave Talia just then. We had unfinished business that I knew could change the course of both of our lives. But, the clans needed me. There was no other way. With each step I took, I prayed what Bo had said wasn't true. Except, I knew in my heart that it was.

It's Ansel. Rafe, your father's come down with this thing. It's bad. It's very bad.

Bo had said other things, but none of it mattered. Ansel was sick. Even if Bo's tone of voice hadn't conveyed the gravity of the situation, something inside told me it was true. Ansel was ancient by bear shifter standards. Younger, stronger bears had already died from this sickness. Time was running out.

When I reached the county line, the distance I'd placed between Talia and me left a hole in my heart. I felt torn between two halves of myself. Talia was mine. I'd known it since the second I caught her scent in the woods that day as she surrounded herself in shimmering blue light. Her kiss sealed it. She was *mine*. My *Anam Cara*, as impossible as that was. Leaving her behind went against everything in me. But, the call of my clans tugged at me just as strong.

I'd left my SUV in a commuter lot near the highway. Having kept to the woods for so many days, it seemed strange to feel the machinery spark to life as I turned the ignition. The urge to shift and run north burned strong, but even in full bear, the car was faster.

It took half a day of driving, but I reached Wild Ridge by nightfall. The pure air filled my lungs and settled one part of my heart at the same time another part longed to get back to Salt Fork.

Talia can take care of herself. I chanted it as a mantra. Although my head knew it was true, my protective inner bear wanted nothing more than to pull her to my side and keep her safe and warm. She was among her own people. As far as I knew, they had no idea she'd been with me. She was safe. She *had* to be safe.

I headed straight for my father's house, high on the southwestern ridge. Lights glared through the windows and I saw figures moving inside. That alone would have been enough to alarm me. Ansel didn't like visitors. Ever since my mother died, he preferred to keep to himself and only socialize with the rest of the clans when he came down to the longhouse or one of the mines.

The front door opened as I approached and Bo Calvin stepped out. Sweat beaded his brow and he carved a hand through his tousled brown hair. Behind him, Jenna Calvin stood at the kitchen sink filling a pitcher with cool water. Jenna was Bo's mother. She was human, an *Anam Cara* herself. When I stepped over the threshold, Jenna turned. Her eyes misted when she saw me and her shoulders dropped, as though she'd just set down a heavy load. I went to her.

"Thank God," Jenna said. Her blue eyes darted over my face as she lifted her hands to cup my jaw. She went up on her tiptoes and kissed me on the forehead. Jenna had been my mother's best friend. Even though I'd been fully grown when she died, Jenna had promised her she'd look out for me. Today, that promise extended to Ansel as well. "He's been asking for you when he's lucid enough to talk."

My throat burned as I swallowed hard and nodded. Jenna stepped away and looked toward Bo.

"Thank you for being here," I said. "I know the risk it puts you in."

Jenna smiled. "There's no risk to me. So far, not a single non-shifter on the ridge has come down with this. I tried to keep my son away, but you know how stubborn he is."

"Mom." Bo came forward. He leaned against the kitchen counter. "If I'm going to get this thing, I'm going to get it. Enough of the Calvin clan have come down with it and I've been side by side in the mines with all of them. We've all already been exposed. What's going to happen will happen. The least we can do is tend to our own until we can't anymore."

I put a solid hand on Bo's shoulder. His friendship meant everything to me. "I owe you. I know Ansel never would have let anyone else step foot in this house but the two of you, lucid or not. If you hadn't stepped in, he'd probably be dead already. Stubborn as he is he would have just gone out to the woods and let this thing take him before he'd ask for help. God, he didn't even bother to call me when he started having symptoms."

"Rafe, as far gone as he is, I think it's safe to assume Ansel knew he was sick even before you left."

I dropped my head. He was right. Of course he was right. So

much had happened, it felt like I'd been gone for months instead of just over a week. Goddamn Ansel. He should have told me.

"I need to see him," I said. I started to walk out of the kitchen and down the hall toward Ansel's bedroom. Jenna put a hand on my chest to stop me.

"Rafe, you need to prepare yourself. He's not himself. He might say things to you he doesn't mean. Half the time he doesn't even know where he is. He drifts in and out and loses time. An hour ago he thought I was your mother. He thought Bo was Simon's father and tried to go after him. He damn near shifted in the bed. He's so weak though, he thankfully couldn't pull it off. I need to be honest. I truly believe if he tries to shift, it'll kill him. His body can't take it. So, whatever you do, try and keep him calm. Don't argue with him or try to confront him. Agree with whatever he says or just don't say anything at all."

I leaned down and kissed Jenna on the top of the head. "I get it. I'll watch it with him."

I shot a look toward Bo. His worried expression did nothing to ease my own fears. I knew Bo well enough to understand there was something else putting that look on his face, more than just Ansel's condition. I ran a hand over my face and squared my shoulders.

"Okay. Out with it. What else is going on I need to know about?"

Bo put a hand up. "Just see to your father. Like Mom said, he's been asking for you. Hopefully, it'll ease his pain a bit. After that, we need to go to the longhouse. A full clan meeting has been called. I've managed to put them all off until you got back."

"Put them all off of what?" Dread snaked its way through my veins.

Jenna stepped between us, putting a flat palm on Bo's and my chests. "Enough, you two. Clan business can wait. Ansel comes first."

I squeezed Jenna's hand and stepped away. Locking eyes with Bo one last time, I turned and headed down the hallway.

The house smelled different. Sickness lingered in the air and settled all around me. With each step I took closer to my father's bedroom, anxiety filled me. A sliver of light spilled into the hallway where his doorway stood half open. I hesitated, hovering my fingers over the doorknob before I finally took a deep breath and pushed my way in.

Ansel already looked dead. He lay on his side, his arm draped over the bed. God, it had only been a week, but he looked like he'd dropped twenty pounds. His skin hung slack over his cheekbones and had a gray pallor that stabbed fresh fear into my heart. His chest rose and fell with unsteady breaths that took way too long in between.

I went to him, sinking into a squat on the floor beside him. I was afraid to put my hand on him, as if just that light touch might cause him agony he didn't need. He wore a white t-shirt that hung off of him, sagging low at the collar. I could see the pox marks covering the front of his chest.

"Dad? Ansel?" I whispered.

He opened his eyes. His bear glimmered just below the surface as his pupils darkened then widened. He struggled to focus and ended up rolling to his front, his body seized by hacking coughs. I put a hand on his back to keep him from falling off the bed. His shoulder blades stuck out, sharp as a knife point. Gently, I rolled him back and peered into his face.

"Dad?"

He reached for me. At first, his eyes glassed over, but when he touched my face, they flared with recognition and his cracked lips curved into a smile.

"You're back. Sweet heaven, I knew you'd come. Did you do it? Did you find that filthy witch responsible for all of this?"

My heart lurched and I swallowed past a lump in my throat. I couldn't decide on the best course of action. Should I lie and give him false hope so he could maybe rest easier? Or should I tell him the truth knowing it would be the same as telling him he had a death sentence? As it turned out, it didn't matter what I said. My father was in there enough to read everything in my eyes. He closed his slowly and let out an unsteady breath.

"Well, fuck, son. I was hoping for better news."

"It's not over yet, Dad. I've got a lead. I may have found someone who can help us. I just need you to hang in there. Do whatever Jenna tells you to. She's got a knack for healing. Get some rest. They've called a clan meeting down at the longhouse. It won't take long. As soon as it's over I'll be back. Don't worry about anything. We're going to find an answer to all of this."

"Twenty men," he whispered. "That's the count. Did Bo tell you that? Twenty have died. Thirty more are sick. At this rate, the ridge will be wiped out before the end of the summer."

My heart froze inside my chest. No, Bo hadn't given me the numbers. I assumed that was part of what the clan meeting was about.

"You just worry about you. Leave clan business to me."

"Son, you're missing the point. We thought the Alphas had been spared. None of 'em got sick. That's why Jenna didn't throw a bigger fit when Bo came down here with her. But I'm still an Alpha, even if you're head of the clan now. I'm glad you're here, but I wished you'd been able to stay away. It'll kill me twice if this takes you out too."

I put a firm hand on his shoulder and pressed him against the pillow when he struggled to sit upright. "It's *not* going to take me out. It's not going to take you out either. I told you, I didn't come back completely empty-handed. There's a witch that I think I can convince to help us. I just need a little bit more time. There's a lot to tell you, but now's not the time. You need your rest. I'll head down to the longhouse and fill in the others. Then, I'm coming back to sit with you. For now, I need you to trust me, okay?"

My father started to cough again. He struggled to say something else, but it was no use. The racket he made drew Jenna's attention and she hovered in the doorway with her hands folded.

"I think he's had enough for one night. Bo's already headed up to the longhouse, Rafe. Why don't you go on after? I have things under control here with Ansel. Come back when you can."

I leaned in close and kissed my father's head. Turning to Jenna, I gave her a grim nod and squeezed her shoulder as I passed her. She lifted a hand to cover mine. She didn't need to say anything else. We'd be lucky if Ansel survived the night. Steeling my back, I grabbed my jacket and headed out the front door.

⚮

THE CLANS WERE IN TURMOIL WHEN I ARRIVED. THE NUMBERS my father had reported were outdated. Since the night before last, another five men had died and ten more had developed symptoms. The sickness was spreading fast. Every single clan had lost men.

When I walked into the conference room, all eyes turned toward me with hope. I chewed the inside of my lip and tried to keep my face even.

I took my seat beside Bo. Simon sat directly across from me and the haggard lines around his eyes alarmed me. Perhaps my father was right; if he could come down with this sickness, maybe no Alpha was safe.

"Dillan Gentry died an hour ago," Simon said with no preamble. My heart sank. Dillan was another of Simon's cousins. With the loss of Pete before I left, his crew had been slowly decimated. This couldn't go on.

Cullen James leaned forward, clasping his hands together he looked at me with desperate eyes. "Rafe, tell us what you found out in Salt Fork. For the love of God, please let it be good news."

The warring halves of my heart tore at me. Before I even said a word, I knew with a growing sense of dread how this would go. A fierce protective instinct ignited inside of me over Talia. I had to make them understand.

"I have a lead," I said, wishing I could muster a less grim tone. But, seeing Ansel like that had truly gutted me.

"A lead?" Simon growled his words. "It better be a damn good one, Rafe."

Bo put a hand up, he threw a look to Trevor seated next to Simon. Trevor moved to grab Simon by the shoulder. I think he meant it as a comforting gesture or at least one of solidarity, but Simon's stiff posture and glinting eyes gave Trevor pause.

"I have an in with the coven," I said, realizing that wasn't really the right way to describe it. But, it was as good as anything else. Talia hadn't agreed to help me, but I knew in my heart that her own instincts about me tugged at her the way mine did for her. It was a start. I just hoped it wasn't too little too late. "There's a woman. I think she'll be willing to help us."

"You think? Jesus, Rafe. Do you need me to spell out for you how dire things have gotten while you've been off on your little camping adventure?"

"Simon," Cullen leaned forward. "Let's hear Rafe out at least."

At least? I looked around the room again. My heart sank as I noticed the hardened stares I got from every other clan leader. Cold dread washed over me as I realized something had happened among the Alphas while I was gone. There was more they weren't telling me.

"I've made contact with one of the witches," I said. "I have reason to believe she could be an ally. I've been careful about what I've told her, but she's working on a healing spell."

Simon pounded a fist against the conference table. "No more spells. I'd rather mercy kill every infected member of my clan before I'd let more vile witchcraft into their bodies."

I wanted to hate Simon for everything he said. Just a month ago, I might have shared his sentiment. But Talia had changed me in ways I didn't fully understand yet. Still, Simon's son had been kept from him for years all due to a witch. He wasn't in a place where he could forgive that, and maybe he never would be.

I put up my hands in a gesture of surrender aimed at trying to placate him. If it were Simon alone, I might have stood a chance. But, looking around the room, I saw those same hard stares. These men had already made their minds up about something. I had maybe one chance to convince them otherwise.

"She's an *Anam Cara*," I said even as my heart flared a warning. *Protect her. Keep her safe!* Simon's eyes flashed along with Cullen's and Jax's. They understood. The *had* to understand. The three of them had taken mates of their own. They knew the war I fought within myself over loyalty to them and to her.

"Then you aren't thinking clearly." That Jax uttered these words made me realize I'd been doomed before I even walked in the door.

"The hell I'm not," I fumed. "I've just come from Ansel. You think I won't do anything in my power to try and save him? I just need a little more time and I know it's in short supply."

"Where's the witch now?" Cullen asked.

I steepled my fingers beneath my chin. I loved these men. I would die for these men. But I wouldn't betray Talia to them.

Seeing my expression, Cullen's eyes dropped and he let out a breath. He understood.

"Fine," he said. "But Rafe, she's a witch. Hasn't it occurred to you that she's used a spell on you to make you *think* she's an Anam Cara? She's a *witch*. That would make a hell of a lot more sense than what you're suggesting. It just doesn't work that way."

"Doesn't it? You of all people know exactly how it works. We don't choose. It chooses us."

My heart dropped and cold rage bubbled along my spine. I looked around the room. Even Bo cast his eyes downward when I tried to meet his gaze. I'd already lost, it seemed.

"We need to take a vote," Trevor said.

"A vote?" My voice came out hard.

Bo put a hand over mine and I jerked mine away.

"We need to take matters into our own hands. It's been worth your effort for recon or even to try diplomacy, but we're past that. If the witches won't help us willingly, we need to remind them of the consequences of going up against us. There's no other choice. Too many lives are at risk," Bo said.

"You realize what you're saying," I said, my voice tasting bitter in my throat. "If we charge into Salt Fork lands and force this, it'll be considered an act of war against the witches. Every man here understands that they're not without power. They'll defend themselves. Look what they've done to us already."

Simon met my eyes. "They've already declared war on us. Have you found out anything that leads you to believe this sickness is anything other than witchcraft?"

"No. But for all we know, it was one rogue witch acting alone. I'm asking you to let another witch try and undo it. If we go to war with them, we'll also lose men. Give me two days. Give the girl a chance to come up with a solution. Once we go down this path, we can't walk it back."

"They're the ones who've started this," Jax said, his voice booming. "You're asking us to sit back and let our people get picked off."

"I'm not. I'm asking you to take one last shot at stopping this before we resort to open warfare with the witches."

"You know damn well what Ansel would say if he were sitting at this table," Trevor shouted.

I rose. White rage clouded my vision and my bear stirred. I clawed my fingertips into the wood. "Ansel is *not* sitting here at this table. He doesn't speak for Clan McCormack. I do. And my vote is to wait forty-eight hours before making a decision that could put us at even greater risk."

"I vote we act now," Jax said. Simon and Trevor joined him. That left Bo and Cullen still to vote. I focused on steadying my wildly beating heart. Every instinct I had called on me to shift right there at the table.

In the end, we were at a draw with Bo and Cullen siding with me. The compromise was simple. Twenty-four hours. They would give me twenty-four hours to see if Talia had anything that could help us. If she didn't, we'd send a contingent onto Salt Fork lands and demand a meeting with the leaders of her coven. It meant war.

Chapter Nine

Talia

"Are you sure everything's all right?" My father sat at the head of the breakfast table spinning his fork into his eggs. His hazel eyes softened as I looked up at him.

Scooting my chair back, I dabbed my napkin at the corner of my mouth. "I'm fine. Promise."

"Well, you don't look well."

"Garrett!" Grandma Torre clanked her knife against her plate. "Not the most tactful thing to say to a pretty nineteen-year-old girl."

"Well, this pretty nineteen-year-old girl also happens to be my daughter, Ellen. And I'm going to bring up the elephant in the room. Talia, you haven't looked well ever since you declared. Your color's off. You seem even more fidgety, not calmer. It's supposed to be the other way around."

"I'm really okay, Dad." I lied. The truth was, in the twenty-four hours since Rafe took off, it had been literally hard to breathe. I felt like I had an anvil sitting on my chest and my legs itched to run. I could lie to everyone around me and even to myself. But, I knew exactly what direction my legs wanted to take me. North. To Wild Ridge or wherever Rafe was. It was ludicrous.

"Well, maybe you need to stay away from the woods for a few days. Give things a chance to settle."

"Dad, I'm *fine*. Really."

"She's a fire mage, Garrett," Grandma said. "I gotta admit I didn't quite see that one coming. You of all people ought to remember what it feels like to declare fire. I sure as hell wouldn't know."

This was a running debate between them. Grandma Torre...*all* the Torres were earth witches. They were calmer, more easygoing. For years I'd told myself I would miss my mother most the day I finally declared. I did miss her, but the simple fact was, she couldn't have helped me a bit with this transition.

"You should spend some time with me down at the forge," Dad said, throwing his own napkin on the table. "You might actually have a knack for it now. It's always helped me when things started running a little hot inside of me. Toby's coming down this afternoon to help me with a new order. It'll do you some good to see how he works. You're more compatible than you realized."

My stomach churned at the implication. Someday very soon I'd have to set him straight that Toby and I were never going to happen.

"You know, I actually wanted to spend some time studying," I said. "Now that I better understand where my power comes from, I'd like to take a look at more fire spells I can try."

"You just be careful with that," Grandma rose and started clearing plates. "You try to do too much too fast and you're liable to burn the damn house down."

CURSE OF THE BEARS

"I'm telling you, that's why the forge is the best place for you right now, young lady."

I took the plates from my grandmother and stepped around my chair. Leaning down, I kissed my father on his bald head. He let out a gruff noise, but smiled. "I promise I'm not going to do anything crazy. And I *will* spend some time down at the forge tomorrow. Cross my heart."

My heart skipped as I waited for Grandma and my father to leave the kitchen. Dad would be gone for at least twelve hours at the forge today. It was Thursday, and Grandma had an honest-to-God knitting circle on the other side of town. It would give me a long stretch of uninterrupted time to do exactly what I said I would: spend time with our existing spellbooks down at the private library on the outskirts of town.

As soon as my father and grandmother left for the day, I grabbed a notebook, packed a lunch, and practically ran the ten blocks from the Purple House to the library. To anyone passing by, the building looked abandoned. Wine-colored ivy covered one side of the square, brick building with the flat roof. For what was contained inside, some might think we'd have armed guards surrounding the place. But, we didn't need it. Circean magic kept the building secure.

My heart jackhammered behind my breastbone as I made the slow walk up the rickety white steps. I'd been inside this building exactly two times in my life and never alone. Only those witches who declared could breach the front door. Anyone else would be turned away unless escorted in by a true witch. Now, *I* was a true witch. Still, as my fingers hovered over the doorknob, I waited for some cold shock or force that might drive me backward and deny me entry. But, the door opened wide and I pressed my way in.

Long ago, this building had been a one-room schoolhouse. All that remained of it was an ancient chalkboard along one wall and three rows of wooden pews. We didn't need rows of bookshelves stretching to the ceiling. The grimoires and spellbooks we shared were simple. This was one of only four Circean libraries in the world, each connected by ley lines. I could call up any text accessible to covens all over the globe with just a simple swipe of my hand.

A thousand years ago, Circean witches had been careless with their treasures. That mistake had cost us dearly. We lost the old magics and the old languages when the shifters came and burned them to the ground.

I swallowed past a hard lump in my throat as I called down the book I needed. It was green with frayed edges and a loose binding. My mother had shown it to me. She warned me the most powerful healing spells were hard to cast and usually took too much out of the caster to do any good. "But someday, someone I love might need one badly enough to make it worth it," she'd said.

I found the spell and smoothed my hand over the pages. My magic stirred and I smiled. This *was* a fire spell. My nerves thrummed and my body itched to say the words out loud. But now wasn't the time. A spell as powerful as this one would be strongest the first time I cast it. I couldn't waste it. I took a deep breath and hovered my hands over the ancient text. Just a few days ago, the words would have looked like gibberish to me. Now, they made perfect sense. As I exhaled, the words faded on the page then disappeared. The spell was in me now until I cast it. Only then would the words reappear on the page. The spell wasn't mine to keep, only to borrow.

My blood heated with the power of the magic. I stilled my thumping heart and smiled. I wasn't foolish enough to think that one spell alone would help the shifters if the source of their sickness truly was witchcraft. To undo that, I'd need to find the witch who cast it. Then, they'd have to willingly undo it. If they *weren't* willing, the spell could only be broken by the death of the caster. A chill ran through me at what that would mean. I tried to push those thoughts aside. If indeed there *was* a witch from our coven who'd done something to hurt the shifters, she'd have to face the entire coven. The last witch who'd done that was my aunt.

The memory burned strong through me. Last year, I'd been sent along with two other women from the coven to try and bring her back into the fold after the coven caught wind of her using black magic. I'd begged my father not to send me. I had no magic of my own yet. But, I shared Aunt Gwendolyn's blood. To have any hope of controlling my aunt if she put up a fight, the coven needed me to complete their circle. I knew my father and grandmother secretly hoped the process would jumpstart something in me and get me to declare. It hadn't worked. Aunt Gwendolyn *did* put up a fight. The pain of it still echoed in my fingertips. We'd killed her. There had been no other choice.

My fingers trembling. I closed the healing spellbook and called forth the book my mother told me never to touch.

"There's a place for dark magic," she'd said. "You should never be afraid of it. It's when witches try to twist it to serve their *own* ends things can take a turn, Talia." That's exactly what Aunt Gwendolyn had done. She'd used her magic against another shifter. We were lucky to stop her without starting a war.

The book appeared in the corner of the table. It was smaller than the others, barely more than the size of a prayer book. It had the look of one too with gold-trimmed pages and a black leather cover. I reached for it and started thumbing through the pages.

Most of the spells didn't seem all that terrible. I found love spells, growth spells, more minor healing spells. If I didn't know any better, I would have assumed this was just a normal spellbook filled with harmless white magic. Except the more I read, the colder the room got. Every single spell in this book was designed to make something happen against another being's will. The air grew thick and it got harder to breathe. Still, the book compelled me. Faster and faster I flipped through the pages. I didn't even know what I was looking for. Surely I wouldn't find something as obvious as a spell labeled "Shifter Killer." Anything that powerful would have likely been lost when the old libraries were burned to the ground. They say that's exactly what the shifters had been looking for.

My heart felt like it turned to ash when I reached the final page. What I found there made my stomach churn. Or rather, what I *didn't* find there. A spell was missing. The last ten pages of the book were blank, but the smell of smoldering magic still lingered. There *had* been a spell here written in bold black lettering like all the others. But, someone had taken it just like I'd checked out the healing spell in the green book.

It could have been anything. Maybe it was a minor hex against a jilted lover. Except, I knew in my heart it wasn't. Somewhere out there, a witch from our coven had taken a dark spell and was walking around with it right now. Would I know him or her if I saw her? Was it enough to get the full coven to intervene?

I didn't have a chance to ponder it any further. The wind kicked up outside and the hairs prickled along the back of my neck. A strong urge settled low in my gut. I stumbled backward, knocking my chair over as I gasped for air.

Rafe.

He was close. I sensed him moving fast. He was headed for the cabin. In that moment, I knew no power on this earth would keep me from meeting him there. I stacked the books on the corner of the table and headed for the door. Though I didn't have much to go on, at least I had something. Maybe if I knew more about the sickness plaguing the bears, I'd be able to recognize the trace of magic that produced it. Just *how* I'd get that information sent a stab of heat through me. But, there was no time to worry about that now. I had to get to Rafe.

Before I made a conscious choice to do it, I found myself racing toward the woods. I took the back alleys on the outside of town. My heart and my magic pulled me forward. Desire flooded through me with each step I took that would bring me closer to Rafe. My God. He was right. I hadn't wanted to believe him, but in my heart I knew it was true. My magic connected me to him. I couldn't deny it.

Branches pulled at my hair. I tripped over a rotted tree stump but kept on running. It made no sense, but I could swear I felt Rafe's heartbeat thumping inside my own chest. He was so close.

I was almost there. The cabin was half a mile away. I didn't feel the chill in the air or even my legs. If I tried, I wondered if I could fly. But wind wasn't the nature of my magic, so my feet stayed rooted to the ground. I stumbled into the clearing and would have called out Rafe's name. Something grabbed me from behind and turned me around, wrenching my arm so hard it nearly dislocated.

Staggering sideways, I righted myself and looked up. Toby towered over me, his fingers digging into my upper arm; he pulled me back.

"Where the hell do you think you're going, Talia?"

Out of breath, my stomach roiled as I struggled for solid footing. Toby held me tight. Reaching with his other hand, he gripped my shoulders hard and shook me.

"What's he done to you?" he demanded.

"What are you talking about? Let me go!"

"You think I don't know what you've been up to? You think I didn't sense his filthy presence all over you the other day? God, Talia. You reeked from it."

My mind spun. He knew. Somehow, Toby knew. Every instinct inside of me told me to lie, deflect, protect Rafe. Menace made Toby's eyes flash dark. His own fire magic simmered just below the surface, making his fingers crackle with lightning.

I tore myself away from him, pushing out with my own power. Toby took a step back then advanced on me again.

"You don't know what you're talking about, Toby. Go home. What I do is none of your damn business."

"What you do is *everyone's* business, Talia." He reached into his back pocket and pulled out his phone. He swiped the screen and turned it toward me. The image was grainy and from a distance, but he had a picture of me. It was Rafe and me. Oh, God. It was from the other day right after Rafe shifted. He was lying on top of me and we were kissing. Rafe was naked.

"Give me that!" I reached for Toby's phone. He held it up and away from me.

"Fucking whore," he spat. "A bear, Talia?"

"You don't know what you're talking about," I said. "You don't have the first clue. Go home, Toby. Just go home."

My mind reeled with the thousand things that could happen if and when Toby decided to tell anyone else what he'd seen.

"You're just like your aunt," he said.

"No! I'm nothing like her. Toby, if you've ever valued our friendship, I'm begging you to keep this to yourself for now. I need you to trust me. What's happening isn't what you think it is. If you show that to anyone before I have a chance to explain, it'll be a disaster for the whole coven. You have to trust me."

He slapped me. He moved so quick I didn't see it coming. His palm smacked across my cheek and stung me. I staggered sideways and blood filled my mouth.

"You're done, Talia. You've broken the treaty. You've violated the coven. You might not care about what that means, but I do. Now pull yourself together, we're going back to town. You're going to answer for what you've done."

Rage clouded my vision. My fingers curled into fists and hot lava seemed to flow through my veins. The sky darkened and thunder rolled in the distance. Static electricity made my hair stand on end, and when I looked up, Toby's eyes widened and I could almost taste the fear behind them.

I spat blood at him, hitting him in the shoulder. I was quick, but Toby was quicker. I should have known he would be. My magic was strong, but he had more control of his. When I raised my hand to drive him backward, he was ready for me. My light bounced off of him and he countered with his own. It knocked me square in the chest and right off my feet.

Toby stood over me, his eyes swirling blue light as his magic gathered strength. He reached down and jerked me forward, digging his fingers into my shoulder. I kicked at him, trying to get my arms up to knock him back again.

Thunder cracked and a shadow moved across Toby's face. Then the ground trembled and a growl erupted, loud enough to shake the branches all around us.

Rafe's bear ripped through the tree line with the force of a hurricane. He stood with his front paws over me, shielding me from

Toby. Toby staggered backward as Rafe bared his teeth and twisted his great head. I put my hands up to cover my ears as Rafe's growl filled my body.

"Stop!" Toby cried. He got his hands up and lightning danced between his fingertips. Rafe never let him get the chance to channel it. He swiped one great paw and knocked Toby sideways. Toby hit a tree and the bones of his shoulder cracked. He cried out in agony and slid to the ground.

He was going to kill him. Rafe's bear lumbered forward, his breath coming in great, chuffing pants.

"Stop!" I had the presence of mind to scream. "Rafe! No!"

If he killed Toby, the coven would never listen to me. They'd only see a witch killed by a shifter. There'd be no turning back.

I scrambled to my feet and put a hand on Rafe's back. My fingers sank into his thick fur.

"Rafe!" I gasped. "Let him go. You have to let him go."

The bear's head loped, swinging wildly; he looked at me. Those great black eyes searched mine with keen intelligence. He heard me. He understood me. Growling, he looked back at Toby.

"Run," I said. "Do you hear me, Toby? Get up and run!"

Clutching his ruined shoulder, Toby made it to his feet. His wild eyes looked from me to the bear and back again.

"You can't stop this, Talia. The coven already knows. Fucking whore. You brought all of this on yourself. You're the one who'd better run, bitch."

But Toby got his legs beneath him. Spit dangled from his lip as he gasped for air. Then, Toby turned and ran toward town, leaving me alone with the bear.

Tears filled my eyes and I sank my fingers into Rafe's soft fur. I pressed my forehead against his side and started to sob. His fur bunched and rolled then receded. As I clung to him, Rafe shifted back. His paws were gone and he encircled me with strong arms.

"Are you all right?" he said through ragged breaths.

Nodding, I wiped my eyes and looked up at him. His eyes filled with unspeakable tenderness as he put a gentle finger along my jaw. It ached and I could feel it starting to swell where Toby struck me.

"He hit you."

I shook my head. "I'll be all right."

Except I wouldn't. Even as I said it, I felt a fresh charge in the air. Lightning. Magic. And none of it belonged to me.

"We can't stay here," Rafe said, sensing the change himself.

Sniffling, I smoothed my hair back and nodded.

"They're coming. The coven. If they find you here, they'll kill you. God knows what Toby's already told them."

Swallowing hard, Rafe nodded. "That's exactly why I can't leave you here. Come on."

Before I could answer, Rafe scooped me up in his arms. With a powerful magic that took my breath away, he shifted mid-stride and deposited me on his back. I dug my fingers into his fur as his bear let out a roar then took off at a full run while I held on for dear life.

Chapter Ten

RAFE

Talia wrapped her legs around me as I picked up speed. My vision darkened as my bear ran free. I would have kept running if Talia hadn't shouted. We'd left the cover of the woods and the highway loomed just up ahead. She dug her heels into my side and I splayed my paws wide, carving them into the soft earth and braking.

I dropped to all fours and shifted, forcing the bear still inside of me. We'd reached the side of the road. My SUV was parked a few yards to the south along the berm.

"Come on," I said. "We'll be faster on wheels than on foot."

Gasping for air, Talia nodded. The angry welt along her cheek made the rage churn inside me again. He'd touched her. Her pain exploded inside my brain the instant that asshole made contact. I reached for her, running a gentle thumb along her jawline. She pressed her hand to mine and managed a weak smile.

"It's nothing," she said. "I could heal it myself in about thirty seconds, but I don't know what's coming our way. Better to save every ounce of magic I have."

Nodding, I pulled her close. Threading my fingers through her hair, I kissed the top of her head. Never again. If I had the power to stop it, I'd never let anything touch her again. I opened the back of the SUV and pulled out a change of clothes, dressing quickly.

"We need to move," I said. I could still sense a gathering menace north of us, just past the state park. I took Talia's hand and helped across the steep embankment on the other side of the car door. She slid in the passenger seat and I came around the driver's side. I gave her a tight-lipped smile as I turned the ignition.

"Where will we go?" she asked, sliding her seatbelt into place.

"I guess south. We need to put some distance between you and Digby."

I felt fear flare in Talia. I wondered how many times she'd actually left her hometown. Certainly she'd never left it not knowing when and if she could return. I longed to take her to Wild Ridge, but that was out of the question for the moment too. With the clans itching for war, I couldn't guarantee her safety. She shot me a look as if she could read my thoughts. It occurred to me I didn't know for sure whether she could. I slammed the car into reverse, spun us around, then hit the gas heading away from Salt Fork.

I drove as if the car were fueled with hellfire rather than gasoline. I wasn't entirely sure Talia's magic wasn't partially at play. But, she kept her fingers folded in her lap, her forehead pressed against the window.

I don't remember making a conscious choice about where to go. I just knew I needed to put as many miles as I could between her and her people...and mine. I headed southeast. A different wilderness called to me and I'll never know whether that was predestined either. But, hours seemed to pass like minutes as we headed for the mountains.

By late afternoon, we'd crossed the Virginia border. We ran out of gas on the edge of the George Washington and Jefferson National Forest and that suited me just fine.

Talia didn't question me. I slung my backpack over my shoulder, parked the car against a guardrail, then came around to the passenger side. I opened her door and held out my hand. Talia's eyes searched my face. Her cheek had started to bruise. She looked at me with trust and wonder, then took my hand and slid out of the car.

We hiked deep into the woods. Talia's step never faltered and she kept pace with me despite the wild terrain. She seemed as at home here out in the wild as I did. It was where I found her, after all. My own magic called strongest to me out in the open like this and I sensed hers did too. Maybe shifters and witches had more in common than I'd ever let myself consider.

We hiked for two hours, saying little to each other besides directions. I let instinct guide the way. I hadn't planned how long we'd travel, but soon I found a small cave nestled near a hidden lake. It was perfect.

"Let's make camp here," I said.

She put a hand on her hip and scanned the horizon. She tilted her chin toward the wind and closed her eyes, inhaling deeply. Though she'd kept up with me all afternoon, her shoulders sank with relief at the promise of rest. Still, lines of worry creased her face and she kept her gaze focused on some distant point. I lifted my nose but didn't smell anything I couldn't deal with.

"What is it?" I asked. "Are they coming?" Soon, I'd need to ask her hard questions about the coven's powers. I had no idea how well they could track her or whether Talia remained connected to them.

Her eyes snapped open. She fixed them on me. "Not yet. But, they will."

I put one hand on her shoulder and hooked a finger beneath her chin. "No one is going to hurt you as long as I'm with you. I swear that on my life."

Her green eyes glistened. There was just enough daylight that I could see her features clearly. My exotic beauty. She reached up and touched her hand to my cheek.

"I wish I could promise you the same thing...bear."

I smiled. "Come on. You've got to be starving. I'll make a fire and catch you a fish."

Talia pulled away from me. "How about you just catch the fish. Fire is *my* specialty, remember?"

She stepped around me and headed to the clearing nearest the lake. Talia gathered a few small twigs, rubbed her hands together, then dropped a spark on the pile of kindling she'd made.

"Not bad," I said, impressed. She gestured toward the lake. It was my turn to impress her. I pulled the string and pole out of my backpack. Within a few minutes, I'd caught a handful of perch. By the time I made it back to the campfire, Talia had already found the small iron skillet out of my pack. She took the catch from me and made quick work with a fillet knife. Again, I stood back smiling, impressed with her. We ate in uneasy silence, with Talia sitting cross-legged on the other side of the campfire.

Finally, I couldn't hold back the question gnawing at my mind. "How long?" I said. "And how many?"

Talia reared back. Tears filled her eyes and she drew her knees up, hugging them in front of her.

"I don't know how many," she answered. "The whole coven, at least. Toby...that's the guy who hit me. He had a picture of us together. He's probably shown it to all of them by now. My father's going to be devastated."

I dropped my head. "Fuck."

"Exactly."

I went to her and sat beside her. I wanted to wrap my arms around her and draw her to me. I wanted to drive away everything hurting her, but I knew that wasn't possible.

"Why did you leave?" she asked. "That phone call you took at the cabin. Something bad happened. What is it?"

I swallowed hard and struggled with those two opposing parts of myself. I had twin urges to protect the clan at all costs and to protect Talia too. Somehow, I'd need to find a way to do both. But, I was about to ask her to tell me things about her coven that her people might consider a betrayal. In turn, I'd have to do the same for her.

"My father," I finally said. "He's come down with the sickness I was telling you about. It's gotten much worse."

"And you *really* believe a witch did this to your people?"

Something flashed behind her eyes. I sensed instantly that she was holding something back from me. I shifted my weight and drew away from her.

"You really believe that's impossible?"

I could see the same war going on inside her heart. She wanted to protect her people too. She bit her bottom lip and let out a sigh.

"There is something. It's not much...but..."

"Talia. If you know something...you have to tell me. Bears are dying as we speak."

"I don't know. Rafe, I swear to you, I don't know for sure. It's just...I can't...do you realize how hard this is for me? I can't tell you certain things."

My bear rumbled inside of me. Her eyes widened and I knew she could see the darkness in mine. I put more space between us and dug my fingers into the ground. "Yes!" My voice came out with more rage than I meant. "God, yes. I know how hard this is for you. Do you think it's easy for me? This isn't supposed to happen. *We* aren't supposed to happen. My people mistrust yours as much as yours mistrust mine. But, maybe that's exactly why you and I are here together right now. Have you ever thought of that?"

"Fate? Is that what you're going to tell me again? Fated mates or whatever? That's crap, bear. I don't believe it."

"Do you believe what you feel?"

Her breath came hard, making her chest heave. She wore a blue flannel top and a white tank top beneath it. I could see the swell of her breasts and it made my bear stir again; at the same time I wanted to put a wall around my thoughts. Protect the clans, protect Talia. Very soon we'd reach the point where I wouldn't be able to do both. For now, I couldn't stop staring at her chest. Color flushed her cheeks when she caught me looking.

"Did you do this to me?" I asked, hating myself a little for even saying it. But, I had to. Simon and some of the others had been so adamant and with everything that had happened, I couldn't rule out the possibility that even this...what I felt for Talia...might be part of some greater spell.

"Do what?"

I took her hands in mine and pressed her palm against my chest. My heart thundered beneath her fingertips. She trembled and I felt the growing desire flare inside of her too. It changed everything about her. The tiny hairs stood on end along her neck and I sensed the burgeoning heat in her core. Tiny blue sparks danced between the webbing of her fingers and amplified my own desire. A low growl rumbled through me, strong enough to make the ground beneath us vibrate.

"Did you *do* this to me?" I asked her again, struggling to keep the animal inside of me from tearing out.

Talia's lips quivered as she searched my face.

"No," she said, breathless.

"Do you *want* this?" I asked. Because, I couldn't do this. I couldn't be this close to her with wild things all around us and not do something about it. It happened so quickly. A combustion. I could advance or retreat, but I couldn't stay still.

"Yes!" Her voice erupted from her throat. I think her answer came from that same combustion rather than reason. She couldn't deny her nature for another second either. I didn't know how I'd serve both my clans and my instincts. She didn't either. But, at that moment with the stars beginning to twinkle, there was just one thing between us that was simple.

"Yes," she said again, calmer. "God help me, bear, but yes. I want this."

"Good," I said. Then, I kissed her. She kept her hands flat on my chest and sank into it. Her light went into me and boosted the desire flooding through me.

Talia groaned. Her body melded into mine and I gathered her into my lap. Any ounce of self-control I had disintegrated with her touch. I tore at her shirt and slid my fingers beneath her tank top. I found her nipple and tweaked it, making it pebble for me.

"Bear!" she gasped. My body ignited right along with hers.

"Witch," I whispered. "*My* witch."

She reached for me, pulling my shirt over my shoulders. Talia went up on her knees. I put my hands flat on the ground. It mattered in that moment that she take control. I let her run her hands over my naked chest. She kissed a trail along my shoulder. My cock strained against my jeans as she tugged at my belt. I dug my fingers into the soft earth to keep from tearing her clothes off of her. The instant I thought it, the desire for it nearly knocked me over. Yes. I wanted her naked and wild. My claws came out. Biting my lip, I took a steeling breath and quieted that part of the bear. This first part had to be Talia. I had to be sure. She had to take what she wanted.

She did.

Leaning away from me, Talia pulled the bottom of her tank top and peeled it over her head along with her shirt. She sat in front of me naked from the waist up. My eyes raked over her. Her supple skin shimmered in the rising moonlight. Her pert, dark nipples stood on end as the wind kissed them. I reached for her. Leaning down, I ran my tongue along the slope of her breast and teased her nipple gently between my teeth. She threw her head back and gasped. Her breasts bobbed before me as she shook with pleasure and groaned.

Talia went up on her knees and wriggled out of her jeans. She knelt before me in nothing more than a thin pair of cotton panties. Smiling, I slid my hand between her legs knowing full well what I'd find there. My Talia was soaked for me. She shivered beneath my touch and leaned back, supporting her weight on her elbows.

I rose slowly and slid out of my jeans. My cock sprang free and Talia's eyes traveled along the length of it. Her lips parted in anticipation. I laid down beside her, sliding my arm beneath her waist.

"I want to make you mine," I whispered.

She put a tender hand to my cheek. Her eyes sparkled. She said one simple word and it altered my world forever.

"Yes."

I hooked my fingers beneath the crotch of her soaked panties and dragged them down. Talia's instincts took over and she spread her thighs wide. Her swollen sex glistened. I played my fingers over her slick folds and she arched her back for me. Oh, yes. It was as if her body was born for mine. If I had any doubt, they melted away with the single shuddering breath she took as I circled the pad of my finger around her swollen clit. My Talia *was* born for me.

"Please," she moaned. She was so ready, so wet. My cock throbbed and I couldn't wait another second longer. Later, I'd take my time with her. For now, my inner bear took over.

I positioned myself between her legs. Talia wrapped her legs around my waist and threaded her fingers through my hair. She leaned forward and grasped my earlobe between her teeth. One sharp bite and I reared back, growling. She tilted her hips forward. The head of my dick nudged her slick opening. I couldn't contain myself a second longer.

I slid inside of her, sheathing myself deep. Talia gasped. There was an instant of resistance, but as I thrusted again, she opened to me. My God. My Talia. I never asked but should have sensed it. She was a virgin. I threw my head back and let loose a full-throated growl. Her body answered with a rush of juices, guiding my entry.

I clawed my hands into the ground and took her. With each thrust, she cried out for me. First bear, then Rafe. Over and over. I felt her heat rising. She clawed at my back, drawing blood. It was ecstasy. She couldn't have known unless she was made for me. And she was. Oh, God, she was.

Grunting, I pushed myself as deep as I could go. I felt Talia's walls clench around me as her orgasm rose. It thundered through her, shattering her. She let out a primal scream that scattered the birds in the nearest trees. It was right that it happened here in the wilderness. It was fate. She flung her hands out. When they hit the ground, balls of blue flame bounced out of her palms and hit the rocks around us. Smiling, I leaned down and nipped her bottom lip.

My Talia unspooled beneath me. I felt a gush of her juices coat us both as she screamed her pleasure toward the sky. She spasmed with delight, her breasts jiggling as she fucked me with abandon. I guided her, pressing my cock deep inside of her and holding it still so she could ride me from beneath and wring out every last drop of ecstasy. When she lacked the strength to keep her legs wrapped around my hips I kissed her neck and gently pulled out of her.

Moaning, she reached for my face. "That was...oh, God."

A low, wicked laugh escaped my lips. "I need to claim you now, witch."

Her eyes flared with fresh desire as she knew instinctively what I needed. "Oh, yes," she gasped, getting her legs under her again. She turned, presenting herself to me on all fours. The sight of her gaping pussy nearly undid me.

With a gentle hand on her hips to keep her in position, I slid home. Talia cried out with lust as I penetrated her even deeper than before. My nature called to hers again and I plunged into her again. With the wilderness all around us, I fucked her deep and hard. Talia raised her hips to meet each and every thrust. I spent myself inside of her as her magic enveloped us in a blue glow.

She was mine. I was hers. My *Anam Cara*. My fate. Maybe it was some spell that bound me to her, but at that moment under the stars, I no longer cared.

Chapter Eleven

TALIA

It seemed as if twice as many stars came out that night as Rafe made me his. After the first time, I thought I might not be able to move for hours. I'd used muscles I never knew I had before. Draping my legs over his, I slept for a time as he traced lazy circles on my back and smoothed my hair away from my face.

But, I recovered quickly, heat and desire slowly building within me again. Something was happening to me. It felt like more than just lust awakening inside of me as I raised my head and kissed my beautiful bear on the lips. My sex throbbed and a wicked smile played at the corner of Rafe's mouth. I slid my hand over his washboard abs and found him ready for me again. His turgid cock throbbed in my hand as I gently stroked him. His eyes rolled back in his head as I cupped his heavy balls. An answering heat flared between my legs and I couldn't contain the urge a second longer. Somehow, I found the strength to fling my leg over his hip and I mounted him, taking him in as deep as I could.

Rafe threaded his fingers through mine and held me up as I rode him. Flinging my head back, my hair flew behind me like a banner as I fucked him. Bucking and grinding, I felt myself open ever wider for him. I had no idea anything could feel this good. Of course I'd pleasured myself before, but this...this was so good, so right. How had I ever doubted for a second the instinct that brought me to this man?

As I came again, I pulled my fingers from Rafe's and laced them through my hair. It felt like my head might pop off as my orgasm rolled through me in waves. Crackling heat poured out of me and sparks lit the air around us. God, it was so good. I squeezed my thighs around him, wringing every drop as I felt his dick spasm and he sought his own release.

For a brief moment, we were no longer two beings. Joined in body and pleasure, I felt part of the air and the earth around us. Rafe said something in whispered tones, but I couldn't hear it. I felt stronger, more centered than I'd ever felt in my life. In the back of my mind I knew it was something more than physical rapture. It was as if I'd achieved ultimate control and abandon at the very same time.

The Source. *My* source. It was all around me.

I threw my head back and cried out to the sky. I reached for it; opening my eyes, it almost seemed as though I could touch the stars. The world spun along with me as the last gasping waves of pleasure rolled through me. I took in Rafe's pleasure too. His hot seed spilled deep inside of me, filling me, completing the circle.

I dropped my chin and met his eyes. He was right there beneath me, but the ground seemed impossibly far away. Rafe threaded his hands through mine again and I took a gulp of air as my orgasm finally subsided. I closed my eyes. When I opened them again, Rafe had hooked his hands behind his head and his eyes flashed with wonder and a fair bit of amusement.

I grew sheepish and slid off of him, my legs feeling like rubber.

"What's so funny?" I said, hugging my knees to my chest. Rafe shifted his weight; resting on his hip, he smiled at me.

"You don't know what you just did?"

My cheeks flamed and I dropped my jaw. "I'm not an idiot. I know what an orgasm is, bear."

He let out a soft chuckle and leaned forward, planting a solid kiss on my cheek. "So do I, but not one like that. Do all witches levitate when they come, or is that something special?"

The air went out of my lungs in a whoosh. I pressed a hand to my forehead and shook the fog out of my brain. "I didn't...I wasn't. We *levitated?*"

"Yep. About two feet off the ground."

I rested my chin on my forearm and blinked wide. "Well, I can't say as I've ever been in a position to ask anyone, but...my instinct's telling me that's something special."

Rafe sat up. He tucked a strand of hair behind my ear and peered down into my face. "Well, my instinct *knows* that was something special. You're incredible."

So was he. I couldn't help but marvel at the beauty of him. Rafe was perfectly made with fiercely cut muscles that I knew came from years working in the mines. His strong back and chest tapered into a narrow vee at the hips. I reached for him, trailing my hands along the thatch of curls over his chest.

He crawled forward, caging me with his arms planted on either side of me. His kisses were slow and tender, drawing me out as I explored his body. Warmth flooded me as my light enveloped us both. It seemed I couldn't touch him anymore without my magic rolling over the both of us.

"It's different," he said as he leaned back against the cave wall. He held his arms out to me and gathered me between his legs. I pressed the back of my head against the solid warmth of his chest. It felt so easy between us, so comfortable. In the back of my mind, I realized maybe I should feel self-conscious. No man had ever seen me naked before, but being with Rafe like this, it was the most natural thing in the world.

"What's different?"

"You," he said. "Your magic. Something changed. Am I wrong?"

Smiling, I laced my fingers through his, admiring the long, tapered nails. His palms were rough from years of hard work. When I laid my palm flat against his, his fingers stretched several inches longer than mine. They were good hands, strong and beautiful. These were hands that could protect me. I knew with everything that I was he would never raise them to me the way Toby had. I shuddered at the memory. Rafe kissed the top of my head, perhaps sensing where my thoughts traveled.

I turned, looking back to meet his gaze. I lifted my hand and cupped his jaw. "You're not wrong. I *am* different. I feel more centered, somehow."

"Hmm. Can I ask you something?"

I brought my hand down and twisted so I was facing him now. "Yes. But some things might be hard for me to answer."

Rafe nodded. "I know that. It's true for me too. But, tell me what it's like. How does your magic work?"

"You first," I said.

Rafe's expression grew earnest. "It's always there. When we're young, we can't control it very well. A shifter child is a volatile thing. That's why only Alphas mating with *Anam Cara* can produce another shifter. It's up to the Alpha to be there to help a young boy control the wildness inside him so he can't hurt himself or anyone else. But eventually, when we're mature enough to accept it as part of ourselves, it becomes as natural as breathing."

I considered his words. His eyes held a darkness that I knew he wanted to keep from me. I knew shifters believed witches were to blame for near extinction of female weres. I bit my lip and exhaled. He was right. I couldn't deny the roll the ancient covens played in that particular curse. I'd always been taught we had reasons for doing it. We'd lost so much at the shifters hands. But, maybe those wars were so ancient, no one could truly remember who started what. Maybe it was time for it not to matter anymore.

"Do you realize how beautiful you are?" he said as he coiled a lock of my dark hair between his fingers.

"It's not something I hear very often. Most people just think I'm strange-looking. Dark hair, dark complexion. Light eyes. I'm made up of a bunch of parts that don't fit."

"Well, you are strange-looking," he laughed. "But everything about you fits."

"I'm a melting pot. My mother was half-Cuban on her father's side. Part Cherokee on her mother's side. My father's pure Irish. I'd say most people don't know what to make of me."

"I know exactly what to make of you," he whispered, drawing me down for a kiss. "Tell me about your magic, Talia."

Smiling, I dropped my eyes. "I've already told you most of it. I draw my power from fire. I didn't know that until just a few weeks ago. That day in the woods, it was the day I declared."

Rafe cocked his head to the side. "Declared what?"

"It's just what we call it. When a witch comes into her own power for the first time. We call it the Source. It's like...uh...our well of magic. Only true witches can access it. Declaring is the time when a witch is first able to tap into it. There were plenty in the coven who thought I was a lost cause. Nineteen is ancient as far as these things go. I was starting to lose hope."

"The Source. And your source is fire?"

I ran a hand through my hair. "Not *my* source, *the* source. Think of witches and witch magic as spokes on a wheel. The Source is the hub. Declaring is how we connect to it. Our element is where we're positioned on that wheel. I'm just best suited for fire spells. I can use wind, water, and earth, but fire magic is my nature."

"But you don't need a spell to do magic. What happened just now...that wasn't a spell, was it?"

Feeling bashful all of a sudden, I dropped my head and smiled. "Well, there are certain personal powers that a witch doesn't need a spell for. Usually, those that center around our own protection or pleasure. I don't need a spell to defend myself or even heal myself. But, if I want to direct my magic outward, to impact another person or a thing, well, that's what spells are for."

My heart jackhammered inside my chest. Though we'd taken no oath of secrecy, revealing that much...to a *shifter*, no less...there could be consequences.

Rafe's face darkened. "So, the sickness that's infecting Wild Ridge, that had to have come from a spell. I mean, there's no other way. It was on purpose."

I took a deep breath and held it. Finally, I let it out and gave him a slow nod. "Yes. If the virus is magic-based, it would have had to have been a dark spell cast by someone who knew what they were doing."

I tried to keep my face even. Those blank pages in the black spell-book haunted me. The simple truth was, a dark spell *had* been taken. There was no other explanation.

"Can you undo it?" He looked at me with such tender desperation that my heart broke into pieces.

"I don't know." I gave him the most honest answer I could. "I mean, I know I can't undo the original spell. Only the caster has that power. But, maybe if dark magic caused the symptoms, light magic could counter them. Or perhaps at least buy some time."

Rafe gathered my hands in his. He turned my palms up and ran his thumb over the lifeline on my right hand. He used enough pressure to send a shiver of pleasure straight up my spine.

"I know why it took you so long to declare," he whispered.

My body went rigid. The air in the cave seemed to thicken, and even the creatures outside went silent.

"Rafe."

His eyes flicked to mine. A muscle twitched in his jaw as he held my gaze. "Talia. My witch. *My Anam Cara.* Haven't you figured it out yet?"

"I'm trying," I answered, and it came out as almost a sob.

Rafe's soft smile melted me. "Don't try so hard, witch. It's right here in front of you."

He pressed my palm to his lips and kissed me. Heat flooded through me, settling low in my belly. Impossible as it seemed, fresh desire coursed through me again. Soon, I wouldn't be able to contain it. Rafe's bear magic seemed to work on me like a drug. I craved it. I *needed* it.

"Witch...Talia," he said. "I think your magic is linked with mine.

Why else would you first declare the second you touched me? I don't know what it means, but I know it matters. So, I have to ask you something. Something I may not have a right to, but I've got no other choice."

I wanted to kiss him. I wanted to warm my body against his and let him fill me over and over. It was so much simpler than this. Telling Rafe about my powers was one thing; using them in the way he needed was something else.

"What happened when you went home to Wild Ridge?" I whispered my question. "You said your father was sick, but that wasn't all of it. There was something else. Tell me."

Rafe let out a hard breath that flared his nostrils. He kept my hand in his and met my eyes again. "Half of the clans are hungry for war. You have to understand, they think they have cause. Are you absolutely sure this dark spell wasn't sanctioned by your coven?"

The question took me aback. It was in me to flatly deny it. Except, I couldn't. I'd heard no rumors to make me think the coven itself was looking to hurt the shifters. But no, I couldn't swear it on my life. So, I told him that.

He nodded, satisfied with that. "Talia, what happens to you?"

"What do you mean?"

"You said Toby has probably told your coven that you're with me. What will they do to you?"

I slid my hand out of his. Crossing my arms in front of me, I stared back at him. "What will the clans do to you for being with me?"

Rafe raised a dark brow and smiled. "Well, I suppose that all depends on whether you can help us with this virus."

"Is that a threat?"

Rafe's face fell. "God, no. Not from me. No. It's just, it's complicated."

"Well, it's complicated for me too. The truth is, I don't know. There's no precedent for this. I'm hoping I'll get a chance to explain."

A low, guttural noise escaped from Rafe. His bear eyes glinted dark and he moved toward me. "I won't let you go back there without me. It's not safe."

"You think I'd be safer if I took you with me straight into the heart of the coven? Trust me, that's the worst thing I could do."

"That Toby, I may not be a witch, but I saw into his soul. He wanted to hurt you far worse than he did. Talia, he was thinking about killing you."

I shook my head. "He wouldn't...he *couldn't*. Besides, he doesn't have the power to make that choice on his own. Not without the coven."

"He could. And I swear to God I won't let that happen. But, do you mean to tell me there's the chance the entire coven might vote to kill you for being with me?"

A hollow pit formed in my stomach as I stared back at him. "No. I mean...oh, God. I don't think so. I need to talk to my father and my grandmother. I can make them understand. No, I don't have proof, but I believe in my heart that whoever did this thing to the bears was acting alone. I think they'll see that's a far worse transgression than what you and I have done. They don't want a war."

Rafe rose. He paced at the entrance to the cave looking more bear than human. Finally, he let out a mighty growl and pounded his fist against the stone wall.

"I *hate* everything about this. This is an impossible situation. How can I serve you? How can I serve my clan?"

The moment he said it, something settled in my heart. It spread through me with cold certainty. I believed him that fate brought us together. I also believed fate wasn't done with us. I exhaled and slowly rose to my feet. I went to him. Rafe braced himself with his hands against the cave wall. His back hunched, he hung his head low. I came behind him and wrapped my arms around his waist and rested my cheek against his naked back.

"You know what we have to do."

He let out a heaving breath. I kissed him.

"My bear," I said. "You have to take me to them. You have to take me to Wild Ridge." Even as I said it, dread unspooled inside of me. Rafe clawed his fingers into the dark rock. Then, he turned to me and gathered me against him.

"What if you can't help?"

"I don't know that I can. I only know I can try. I took one healing spell. Take me to your father. The least I can do is try."

"He might not let you. They're not exactly keen on the idea of submitting to witchcraft to cure witchcraft."

"Ah, so I see your father is stubborn like you are. Well, someone's going to have to make the first move here."

Rafe growled again. His shoulders bunched and I could feel his shifter magic rising to the surface. Smiling, I looked up at him.

"Did I tell you I hate this?" he said. "All I really want to do is stay here in this cave with you forever. How does that sound?"

"Right now? A little bit like heaven. But, I know you don't really mean that. The clans are calling to you. I can feel it. So, I hate to admit it, but you may be right. Maybe a little of my magic is shifter-based."

"You're amazing. Have I told you that?"

"Mmm."

"Talia, look at me. I made you a promise. I intend to keep it. As long as you stay with me, I'll give my life before I let anything happen to you. Even against the clans."

I pressed my face against his chest and prayed he'd be strong enough to keep his promise. Because at daybreak, I was headed straight into the heart of shifter country and the belly of the beast.

Chapter Twelve

RAFE

They knew we were coming. Even if I hadn't called Bo to warn him, the clans would still have met us at the border to the ridge.

Talia stood straight-backed beside me. Her chin jutting up and defiant, she stood in a defensive posture with her feet planted slightly apart and her hands down, fingers splayed wide. I felt the gathering lightning inside of her.

Now that I'd claimed her, the echo of her magic coiled through me. I could sense when it gathered strength, ready to strike, or when it just simmered below the surface, waiting. I knew she could sense the same thing in me. Just a light touch on my shoulder and she could quiet the bear.

"Easy," I whispered. "Let me do the talking."

"Wouldn't have it any other way," she said, narrowing her eyes at the advancing figure. Bo stepped forward first. He shot a leery glance toward me then fixed his eyes on Talia. My inner bear rumbled, ready for a fight if he got too close to her.

"This isn't what we talked about," Bo said.

"Time for talking's over, Bo," I said. "Talia's here to try and help. We're going to Ansel's."

Trevor and Simon came to Bo's shoulders. Simon's eyes had gone bear dark and his growl echoed through the open space. I put a protective hand on Talia's back. Light sparked from her fingertips and Simon saw it. He shifted instantly, towering over us on his hind legs. His fangs bared, he dropped his head and his breath came hard enough to blow Talia's hair back.

She put her hands up, palms out.

"I'm not here to hurt any of you," she said, her voice strong and sure. Only I could feel the doubt and fear swirling inside of her. She was having trouble controlling the urge to defend herself with fire. I stepped in front of her. If she used magic now, we'd never be able to keep things from escalating. I'd never let them hurt her, but I knew I might have to fight to the death.

Simon's bear pawed the ground in front of us. Trevor stepped forward and put a hand on Simon's back.

"Listen," I said, raising my voice loud enough so that every Alpha could hear. "We're out of options. Talia is here under my protection. I've sworn her my oath. You'll have to tear me apart before I let anything happen to her. We have no other choice. Talia can at least tell us once and for all whether there's witchcraft at play here. And she has a plan to treat Ansel's symptoms. If it works, then she's willing to go back to her coven with what she's learned. She has reason to think if this *is* spell-based, then it's someone acting without the sanction of her people. At this point, we have nothing else to lose. No one here can argue that point, and you know it."

"You're speaking for a witch now?" Trevor spat his words. His eyes flashed dark and with the power of Simon's shift still swirling in the air, I knew how hard it was for him to keep his own bear in check.

"I'm speaking for my clan," I said. "And the last time I checked, Ansel's part of my clan, not any of yours. What I do where my father is concerned is my business alone. If Talia can help him, then you'll know it. If she can't, you'll know that too. But, at least we'll be able to make a decision from a position of knowledge instead of ignorance. That's what's been sorely lacking through this whole crisis and every man here knows it. So, I'm not *asking* for anyone's permission to do what I think is in the best interests of my own clan."

"Bringing a *witch* onto clan lands affects all of us!" Trevor shouted.

Simon's bear was damn near feral. He chuffed and started to pace behind Trevor and Bo. Jax and Cullen hung back, but I could see indecision written all over their faces. If Simon decided to fight, I couldn't say for sure whose side they'd join.

"Do you really think I have the advantage over any of you right now?" Talia said, stepping around behind me. "I'm not going to pretend I'm defenseless, but one witch against all of you? Even if Rafe and I weren't...I'm not suicidal. If you don't want my help, that's on you. But, it seems to me like you don't have too many other options."

My witch. My strong, defiant Talia. I feared for her at the same time I admired the courage it took for her to stand up to a line of keyed up Alpha bears running on fear and centuries old mistrust of everything about her. She was my mate, my *Anam Cara*, but in that moment I realized something even more powerful. I loved her.

"Just Ansel," Jax said. He emerged to the front of the line, folded his arms in front of him, and gave me a hard stare. "I don't like this, Rafe. I don't trust her. You think she's your mate. So, you've claimed her. That's your choice for now. But you know full well there will need to be a reckoning for that and soon. You can't stand there and tell us your choices only impact your clan."

"Maybe so, but Talia's right and we're wasting time. I'm taking her to Ansel. I'll let you know how it works out."

"You won't have to." Simon shifted back. His body trembled as he stayed on his hands and knees. Sweat poured down his back and his eyes seemed glassy as he stared back at me. Fear stabbed through my heart as I realized what I'd missed before. Simon was sick. It was early still, but the telltale marks of the virus dotted his arms.

My eyes flicked to Bo's. He gave me a tight-jawed nod that made my heart turn to stone. I turned to Talia; she saw the same thing I did and her color drained. I put a hand on her arm.

"Come on," I said. "Ansel needs whatever help you can give."

No one stood in our way as we went to Ansel's cabin high on the ridge. Jenna Calvin stood in the doorway with her arms folded. The look of tenderness she gave Talia melted my heart a little. Regardless of what brought them here, Jenna and Talia had something in common. They were both *Anam Cara*.

"The good news is he hasn't gotten worse since you last saw him," Jenna said, stepping aside to let us through the front door. "But he hasn't gotten better. I just pray you can do something for him. He's on borrowed time and he knows it."

Once we made our way through the house, Talia moved with efficient purpose. She gathered her dark locks in one hand and twisted them on the top of her head, tying them out of her face with a rubber band. She paused for a fraction of a second at the threshold to Ansel's bedroom. Then, she set her jaw and stepped inside.

Ansel lay on his side facing us. His arm draped over the edge of the bed and touched the floor. The angry pox marks covered his flesh. Jenna said he hadn't gotten worse but he certainly *looked* worse. His breath came in ragged pants and sweat dripped from his brow. Talia took a towel from the basin Jenna had set on the nightstand beside him. She wrung it out and pressed it to Ansel's forehead.

He was delirious and I think that saved her. In Ansel's fevered mind, he thought she was my mother or Jenna. He couldn't process that a witch sat beside him now. Talia whispered soft words to him I couldn't make out. She kept one hand at his brow with the cool towel and hovered the other over his back. Her fingertips glowed as she pulled back the sheet and surveyed his pox-ravaged back.

"What do you see?" I asked, stepping forward. She shushed me and pressed her hand to his back. Closing her eyes, she murmured words I couldn't understand. As she did it, sweat broke out on her own brow. When her eyes snapped open, they'd gone from green to chalky blue. Shimmering light arced from her hands and danced along Ansel's spine. He recoiled in agony, his bear eyes flashing black.

"Talia?" I stepped into the room. Talia put up her free hand in a stopping gesture. Another bolt of light sparked, hitting me straight in the chest, knocking me two feet backward.

She turned her full attention back to Ansel and laid both hands flat on his chest, pushing him flat. Talia rose and knelt on the bed beside him. Her lips moved faster, foreign words spilling forth. The light from her fingertips went from blue to white and crackled. Talia's hair stood on end as the static electricity went through her.

"Rafe?" Jenna came to my side. "My God, Rafe. What the hell is she doing?"

Ansel's weakened body started to spasm on the bed. He doubled over to his side, racked with coughs. His bear eyes changed from black to red and blood dripped from his ears.

"Stop her! Oh, Jesus! Rafe! She's trying to kill him!"

My own bear flared hot. I had twin urges to protect Ansel and to protect Talia. When Jenna tried to get around me, Talia threw a bolt of power toward her. I grabbed Jenna and pulled her behind me just before it would have struck her in the shoulder.

Talia lifted her hands from Ansel and slid off the bed. She went to her knees on the floor beside him, still chanting. Ansel vomited; white foam formed at the corner of his mouth.

"Talia, stop!" I shouted. "Stop!"

She didn't hear me. Instead, her head snapped back and she looked toward the ceiling. Her eyes had become pearly white orbs. Then, as quickly as she'd summoned the magic, it poured out of her in a blinding flash of silver. Talia slumped to the ground, as if all the bones in her body had liquefied. She curled into a fetal position and Ansel passed out.

"Shit!" I ran to Talia as Jenna ran to Ansel.

I lifted her off the ground and ran with her into the other room. "Talia!" I shook her gently as I laid her on the couch. "Talia, wake up!"

"He's alive!" Jenna shouted. "Fucking hell, he's alive!"

My heart hammered in my chest. Talia was gone. Her skin was ice cold and her eyes rolled back in her head. I smoothed her hair away from her face and pressed my forehead against hers. "Talia. Come back. For the love of God, come back."

I took one breath, then another. I lifted my forehead from hers and peered into her lifeless face. Ready to move her from the couch to the floor, I meant to start CPR. Just as I slid my arms beneath her shoulders again, Talia's body convulsed and she sucked in a great, gulping breath of air.

Her eyes snapped open. A capillary had burst in the right one, rimming her pupil in bright red. But, she was breathing. She rolled to the side and sucked in air, but thank God, she was breathing.

"What happened?" she gasped. "Did it work? Is he okay?"

"What happened? Jesus, Talia. You don't remember?"

She shook her head and curled her fingers around my arms, pulling herself upright. She staggered to her feet and started to stumble toward Ansel's bedroom again. I got an arm around her waist and helped her.

She braced herself in the doorway and watched as Jenna wiped Ansel's brow with a fresh cloth. His eyes were clear and he fixed them straight on Talia. He raised a shaking finger and pointed at her. As weak as he was, his voice thundered through the room.

"Keep that bitch away from me," he shouted.

Jenna shot a pleading look at us over her shoulder. She mouthed the word "go." I put an arm around Talia's shoulder and drew her away, closing Ansel's bedroom door behind us.

"What the hell?" I looked at her. "It looked like you just about killed him."

Talia covered her face with her hands. She was shaking, still weak from whatever spell she'd just cast. She shook her head. "It didn't work. Oh, God, it didn't work."

"What do you mean?"

Letting her shoulders drop in a sigh, she finally straightened and looked at me. "It's witchcraft, Rafe. I felt it. There's no doubt in my mind that whatever sickness your father's got inside of him, it's not natural. It's one of the most powerful spells I've ever felt. I think it's...God...I don't even know how to explain this. It's like it's boobytrapped. I could feel the edges of it where it clings to him. But, the minute I got close enough to try and pry it loose, it just snaked all around me like some kind of inky black poison. I'm so sorry. I don't know how to undo it."

The air went out of me. Talia's distress bled through me. She felt despair and hopelessness and the desperation in her voice left no doubt. We were lost. If Talia couldn't help the clans, we were lost.

As drained as she seemed to be, a new energy flared inside of her. She sat bolt upright and started to tremble. "Rafe? Can you feel that? Can you hear it?"

The hairs on the back of my neck stood on end, but I didn't hear or feel anything other than Talia's shifting mood. Still, her agitation stirred my bear. We heard a great heaving cough coming from Ansel.

"Wait here," I said. "I need to check on him."

Talia gave me a breathless nod as I left her side and went to Ansel's room. He was sitting up with his head between his knees. Jenna sat beside him rubbing his back. She looked up at me and fury lit her eyes.

"She could have killed him, Rafe. What the hell was that?"

"Jenna, I know this is hard for everyone to understand, but that girl out there? She's risked everything to try and help us. Whatever's plaguing Ansel isn't her magic. It's not her fault she couldn't undo it. It's enough that she tried. I'll just have to figure something else out."

"Hurry," Ansel said. He looked up at me through bloodshot eyes. I realized at that moment, I was straight-up out of ideas. I went to him and put a hand on his shoulder.

"Just rest. Hang in there. I'm not giving up yet."

"Rafe!" Talia called from the other room. I gave Jenna a grim nod.

"You'll stay with him?"

Sighing, she nodded. "He's too damn stubborn to let anyone else near him. And I don't like this, Rafe. I don't trust her."

"You don't have to," I said. "But I do."

When Talia cried out, I turned and ran to her. She stood in the open doorway. A fierce wind rattled the windows and made her dark hair fly. "What is it?"

"Can't you feel it?"

"No. You keep saying that. What, Talia?"

She shook her head and closed her eyes. "The spell that's making your father sick and all the others. I don't know why I didn't feel it the moment I set foot here. But, now that I've touched it, I know where it's coming from. It's so strong. It's left a trail."

"What do you mean, a trail?" But, before she could answer, a shudder went through Talia. She doubled over and gripped my arm for support. The instant her flesh touched mine I realized how hot she was. It seared me.

"It's this way!" Before I could ask her what she meant, Talia took off running. She flew down the porch stairs and headed for the woods to the east. Her hair flew behind her as she picked up speed.

"Talia!" I gave chase.

She tore at the low hanging branches threatening to ensnare her. She found a hidden trail and barreled down a steep incline, losing her footing then scrambling up again. Tension poured off of her and her fingers sparked like tiny firecrackers as she sprinted down the hill and headed for the valley in the southeast.

Lightning cracked to the west and pregnant drops of rain started to fall. My heart pounded with alarm as the storm seemed to follow us. I'd been in this place with her before. Her magic seemed to call the fire straight down from the sky. Here, in the middle of the wilderness, she could do real damage. But, when I called her name, she couldn't hear me.

We crossed the border into the Marshall clan lands where Simon lived. I felt the rumble of earth as those loyal to him picked up our presence.

"Talia, stop!"

She did, but not because I called to her. She'd reached the edge of the surging stream that bordered Simon's property. On the other side of it, a young grizzly splashed through the rocks, batting away a trout. He was Tad, Simon's son. At only six years old, Simon and his wife often let him hunt here. It was a safe place where he could let his young bear out and get used to the feel of it.

Talia waded into the stream after him. She turned to me, her face white, lips trembling. She pointed to the young bear. "It's him!"

I froze. Witch fire snapped from Talia's hands. Sizzling energy

CURSE OF THE BEARS

encircled her. She went closer to Tad. My own bear roared to the surface. I dug my fingernails into my palms to try and keep him at bay. If I shifted now, she might not understand me.

"Talia," I said, very slowly. "You need to back away from him and come back toward me. Now."

Talia shook her head and pointed to Tad. He went up on his hind legs and let out a small growl. Simon wouldn't have left Tad alone out here. Dark eyes flashed deeper through the woods. We were surrounded.

"The magic," she said. "The spell that's in your father. Rafe, it's *here*. That bear. You can't see it?"

"No, Talia. I just see Tad."

"But it's all over him. He's ensnared in it like a sticky web. Why isn't he sick?"

"Talia, that's Simon's son. Do you know what happened to him?"

Talia's mouth dropped open. Fear went into her eyes and she shook her head no. I took two steps forward and reached her side. Tad roared another warning and the dark menace surrounding us drew closer.

"Stay away from him!" she cried. Tad came toward me with tentative steps across the rocks. He didn't understand what was happening. He trusted me.

"Don't let him touch you, Rafe. He's the carrier. Oh, God."

Tad growled and raised a paw toward me. Talia let the light flare from her fingertips and hit the ground two feet in front of Tad. It didn't touch him, but it startled him enough that he roared and staggered backward. His stab of fear was enough to bring chaos down the hillside.

Simon's bear came barreling through the tree line followed by a half dozen of his strongest lieutenants. Simon leaped into the stream, putting himself between his small son and Talia.

Talia screamed and put her hands up. Energy crackled all around us and I felt the gathering storm of her magic. Simon went up on his hind legs then let out a fierce roar that vibrated over the rocks and threw Talia back. I got between her and Simon's bear, shoving Talia behind me.

"Stop!" I said. "She's not here to hurt Tad."

But Simon was well beyond understanding my words. He sensed his young son in danger from a powerful witch and he'd fight to the death to protect him. Even from me.

We were surrounded. A circle of threat formed. Seven grizzlies in a blood rage and Talia and I at the center of it. I felt Simon's fevered rage boil over. He wasn't thinking straight. In some back corner of my mind I couldn't blame him for it. He sensed a threat against his child. He had every right to defend him. But, if Talia was right, there'd be nothing left to protect us from the dark magic poor Tad unwittingly carried within him.

Simon advanced. He brought his paw down in a murderous arc. I dodged to the side, taking Talia with me. Unable to contain my own bear a second longer, I shifted. Pushing Talia behind me, I turned to take the full brunt of Simon Marshall's fury.

Thunder seemed to come up from the ground. A vast percussion wave of blue light spread over us, knocking everyone to their knees. But, it hadn't come from Talia. The power came from the hilltop above us.

I pulled myself to my feet at the same time Simon did. Dark rage clouded my vision, but Talia's hand on my shoulder steadied me.

A male witch stood above us. He held one hand to upward, channeling a thick ribbon of lightning straight down from the sky. The clouds themselves seemed to open up at his bidding. Then, he pointed his other hand straight toward us, threatening to unleash the bolt straight into us.

"Oh, God," Talia whispered. "That's my dad."

Chapter Thirteen

TALIA

Rafe's bear growled a low, deadly warning beside me. My fingers sank into the fur covering his massive shoulder. Trying to keep my breath even and my temper cool, I whispered to him.

"Steady," I said. "He thinks you're trying to hurt me."

My father's face was pure fire and fury. I'd never seen him like this before. He stood on the hilltop channeling the lightning. With just the flick of his wrist, he could send a bolt through every bear circling us, including Rafe. Whether it would be enough to kill them, I wasn't sure, but we were deep in bear country. The rest of the clans wouldn't hang back. I could feel them even now, gathering behind us, deeper in the woods. My father would never make it out of here alive.

When I met his gaze, I realized that wasn't his purpose. He saw his only daughter surrounded by six feral werebears, five of whom seemed determined to do me harm.

"Rafe," I said, pressing my forehead against Rafe's shoulder. The powerful muscles went rigid and my whole body lifted off the ground as he let out a great breath. Rafe pawed at the ground and shook his head, making a chuffing noise. I couldn't tell whether he could communicate with the other Alphas, but for now, they stood in a stalemate, recognizing the power my father wielded in his bare hands.

"Rafe," I said, swallowing hard. "You have to let me go to him." The instant I said it, cold fear snaked its way through my heart. Going to my father meant leaving Rafe behind.

Rafe let out a soulful whine and pawed the ground again. Even in his bear, he seemed able to understand my words and thoughts completely. Some calmer, detached portion of my brain wondered if that was normal. An instant later, I learned the mental conduit between us went both ways.

"No!" Rafe's intention transmitted clearly into my head. He fixed his wide, black eyes on mine.

"Talia!" My father's booming voice echoed through the valley. Thunder rumbled to punctuate the clear threat he posed to the Alphas. I was running out of time to de-escalate this.

"Rafe," I whispered, wrapping my arms around his neck. Rafe's thumping heartbeat echoed my own. "I think he's willing to die to protect me."

So am I! Rafe's thoughts slammed into my brain. He nudged me with his snout, pushing me further behind him.

Simon's bear broke from the group. He took three lumbering steps closer to my father, putting his bear cub firmly at his back. He was so young, the cub was oblivious to the trouble he'd caused. The spell surrounding him churned in inky waves. God, never mind my father. The danger the cub posed to the rest of the Alphas was real. It took everything in me not to lash out at the cub and drive him back. Doing so would sign my death warrant. I closed my eyes and tried to steady my breath. The cub was an innocent. He had no idea of the evil he'd brought to the ridge. This was *our* fault, not his. We should have stopped this dark magic sooner.

My father lowered his arm. Lightning bounced off the rocks and hit the ground with the force of a shotgun blast two inches from Simon's front paws. He arched his back and let out a ferocious growl.

"Stop!" I shouted; letting go of Simon, I stepped forward. The other Alphas tried to close ranks, but Rafe pushed forward, keeping them from getting any closer to me.

I turned back to Rafe. "Can't you see? This is the only way. Let me go to my father. I'll get him out of here. There's no good end to this right now. If he hurts the Alphas, he'll never make it out of here alive. Then we'll have bodies on both sides and a war none of us will be able to stop."

You're mine! The force of Rafe's protective rage nearly drove me to my knees. But, I stood my ground and took another step outside the circle.

"Not this way," I said. "This can't end like this here on this ridge. I'm still the best chance you have for a cure if I can get the covens to understand what's happened. You have to quarantine that cub in the meantime. I'll find a way back to you. No matter what."

I didn't wait for permission. I pushed through the Alphas and went toward my father. Rafe growled and tried to give chase. The other Alpha bears closed ranks to stop him. I think Rafe might have taken them all on anyway, but my father let loose another stream of fire, driving them all back.

My heart shredded as I looked back toward Rafe. He rose on his hind legs and let out a plaintive wail that gutted me. Hardening my spine, I turned away and broke into a run straight toward my father.

⚜

A HOLLOW SPACE FORMED IN MY HEART WITH EACH STEP I TOOK away from Rafe and the ridge. My father threw out a protective barrier aimed at keeping the bears from following us, but I knew it was futile. No spell on earth could keep Rafe from sensing me. It comforted me at the same time new fear grew inside of me. If Rafe tried to follow us back over the border, he'd face the entire coven.

As it stood, that's exactly what awaited me as well.

My father said nothing to me until we reached the boundaries of Salt Fork. I expected him to drive straight into Digby, but he had other plans. Instead, he took the turn and slammed the car into park. We were at the mouth of the forest; the trail leading to the tiny cabin where I'd taken Rafe beckoned.

Dad banged the car door shut and strode toward the trail. I sat in the passenger seat wanting to be anywhere else but here. When he realized I hadn't gotten out to follow him, he turned and spread his hands wide in a questioning gesture.

Finally, I got out and went to him.

"Did he hurt you?" my father asked. The question startled me and melted my heart a little. I'd sensed only fury spilling off of him. It was stupid of me to think he hadn't also been scared to death.

"Dad, no."

He turned away from me and headed up the trail. Sparks flew

from his fingertips and hit the ground in tiny explosions of fury. I'd never seen him like this. For a fire mage, my father was mostly calm and even. I realized then there was something to what he'd said about the forge. He'd found a way to channel the darkest parts of himself. I envied him at the same time I faced his fury.

He headed for the cabin and I went after him. Even now, Rafe's presence clung to this place. I knew my father sensed it. He recoiled as he reached for the cabin door and pushed it open. The wind picked up as night fell and I followed my father inside.

He stood with his back to me, his hand on the fireplace mantel. His chest heaved as he tore his other hand through his hair. I searched for the right words to say and realized they'd never come. All that was left was the truth.

"I need you to listen to me with an open mind and forget whatever lies Toby has already spread."

Dad whirled on me. "Toby? Toby said you've lain with a shifter, Talia. Are you going to stand there and tell me that's a lie?"

My heart dropped and turned to ash. I slowly closed my eyes and tried to center myself. When I opened them, my father had sat down on the hearth and buried his face in his hands.

"His name is Rafe," I said. "Rafe McCormack. And his people have been gravely hurt at the hands of a witch from our coven. If we don't do something to help them, we are headed for a Shifter War that will decimate all of us."

"I don't *care* what's happened to them! I only care about you, Talia. Do you understand what you've done? Do you understand what the rest of the coven wants to do to you? My God. I *saw* what those bears were about to do. They would have ripped you apart if I hadn't gotten there in time."

"Well, they don't trust us any more than we trust them. And they have good cause. You can be angry with me. I lied to you and I'm sorry about that. But, you know what's up there in Wild Ridge. You were there. Are you going to stand here and pretend you didn't see that bear cub?"

My father waved a dismissive hand. He shook his head and stared at a point beyond me. But, I knew his face. I shared many of his expressions. He *had* seen the bear cub.

"Dad. That was the cub your sister hid from the shifters. Now I understand why. I don't know how she did it, but Aunt Gwendolyn infected that poor kid with something. It's the darkest magic I've ever seen. It's *killing* the rest of the clans. I tried to heal one of them. I couldn't do it. I don't think anyone can do it until we find a way to break the spell around that little boy."

"You don't know that. You can't be sure my sister's behind this. She's dead, Talia. You were there when she died. Her magic died with her."

"That's right. I was *there* when she died because you *sent* me to her. There's a spell missing from the dark grimoire. You can check yourself if you don't believe me. I don't know, maybe Aunt Gwendolyn had someone else helping her. Maybe she found a way to alter the spell to survive without her. You know there are stories of other witches who did things like that."

My father rose. "Talia, you don't know what you're saying. Those other witches? Those were elders who died a thousand years ago. Do you need me to remind you *how* they died? Shifters murdered them."

I crossed my arms in front of me and glared at them. "Enough! My God, how long are we going to hang on to a feud that ended over a millennia ago? Did you know the shifters say they killed the elders and burned the libraries in retaliation for a curse *we* cast that killed off their women? That curse is *still* hurting them."

"So you're loyal to bears now?"

"No! I mean...I don't. What I'm *trying* to say is that this feud happened so long ago, nobody even remembers who started it or who did what when. It's time to end it on all sides. Right now, the shifters have a pretty damn good reason to come after us. Again, you *saw* that cub. Tell me you didn't sense the black magic clinging to him. He's a baby! And those bears are dying out because of something one of us did. It doesn't matter how or why. There's a war coming if we don't find a way to fix it."

My father dropped his head. He took a great gasp of air. When he lifted his eyes to mine, the fight had gone out of him. I crossed the distance between us and put my head on his shoulders. A tremor went through my father and he closed his hand over mine.

"I can't keep you safe, baby," he said. "I promised your mother I would. I've already lost so much. I can't lose you too."

"You won't. And I'm sorry I kept Rafe from you. You have to understand it confused me too. But, it's fate. I know you don't want to hear that, but it's true. He's meant for me, Dad. It's the only way I can think of to explain it and it's terribly inadequate. I just need you to trust me. And I need you to help me with the coven. We have to make them understand it's up to us to find a solution to the bears' sickness. If we can't, then we're all doomed. Every one of us."

When my father exhaled again, he gave me a slow nod and my heart went to him. He loved me. I knew everything I'd said went against his deepest beliefs. But, it was enough if he believed in me. It meant I had a chance of setting everything right.

Later, after the rain stopped, he said it was time to head back into Digby. He wanted me to stay here at the cabin until he could talk to the coven as a whole and get them to agree to hear me out. I only hoped it wouldn't be too late. Rafe would come for me sooner or later. My heart thrilled at the thought of it. At the same time, I feared for the danger it would put him in.

Dad wrapped his arm around me and kissed me on the cheek. We stood together and headed for the cabin door. When we opened it, the air left my lungs in a whoosh. They'd come cloaked. We should have sensed them all around us, but we didn't.

"Talia," my father said, his voice thick with fear. "Whatever happens, just stay behind me."

It was a noble gesture and I loved him for it. But not even Garrett Lear had the power to protect me from the full force of the coven. They'd come together, all two hundred of them. They formed a circle around the cabin. As my father stepped forward, a cyclone materialized in front of him. It knocked him to the ground and he rolled to the side.

Reaching for him, I cried out. Then, a thunderbolt hit me from the side before I could raise my hands to defend against it. The air left my lungs and a hollow blackness enveloped me before I could even scream.

Chapter Fourteen

RAFE

It took four full-grown shifters to restrain me. My eyes locked with Bo's as he sat on my chest. Murderous rage poured out of me and my bear roiled. If Trevor and Cullen hadn't pinned my claws back, I would have ripped Bo's neck open with a single swipe.

Talia was in danger. She was in pain. She was locked in darkness and I couldn't breathe. I tried one last time to knock Bo off my chest, arching my back and pressing my snout forward. I was so focused on trying to kill him that I didn't see the swing. In the final flash before I lost consciousness, I saw Simon's paw just before it slammed into the side of my head. Then everything went dark.

I woke to cold pain. Icy water slammed into my chest. I heaved and sputtered, trying to get my legs under me. I'd shifted again. I lay naked on a cement floor. Shaking the water from my head, I lurched forward and stood. With growing horror, I realized where I was. They had me in one of the outbuildings near the mouth of the Calvin mines. Bo's territory. We'd built a steel cage in one.

They hadn't been used for decades, but there had been times when wild young shifters needed to cool off where they couldn't hurt themselves.

Another blast of cold water hit me in the face and my claws came out. I rammed the side of the cage, gripping the bars. I yanked hard, but knew it was no use. These bars were built to withstand even shifter strength.

Bo and Trevor stood in the corner of the room. Trevor slammed the empty bucket on the ground.

"Why the fuck did they send *you?*" I said, my voice more bear than human. "You're the only two Alphas on the ridge who don't have a clue what's going on inside of me."

"Right," Bo said, hissing his words as he got closer to the cage. "Because Trevor and I don't have mates. Are you really sticking with the idea that a witch is your *Anam Cara?*"

I slammed my fist against the bars, making it shake and rattle. "She's in danger. She's not safe. That's exactly why they told you two to stay down here with me, isn't it? Because everyone else knows what I have to do. You're all a bunch of fucking cowards."

Trevor stepped forward. He got right in my face but kept enough of a distance that I couldn't reach him. He pulled his shirt open. His skin had taken on a gray pallor and pox covered his chest. I pressed my forehead against the bars and exhaled.

"That's two of us now, Rafe. Simon's getting worse. Your father is barely alive. None of the Alphas were sick before she came. You still really believe she was trying to help us?"

It was in me to rail at him again. Quiet desperation filled me. Talia was in such a dark place. She was tired and scared. My God, I had to get to her. Almost nothing else mattered...almost. I raised my eyes and met Trevor's gaze. True fear filled his eyes. No one had survived the sickness. No one. Some lingered with it longer than others, but every man on Wild Ridge who developed the pox like Trevor had ended up dead.

"Yes," I finally said, willing my voice even. Rage fueled me, but it wouldn't help either of them see reason. "And her name is Talia. She came here knowing full well the risk it took. If her father hadn't shown up when he did, you all would have tried to kill her."

"She went after Tad, Rafe."

"She traced the spell that's causing this to him. Come on, you know we all suspected it before Talia confirmed it. He was under a witch's guard for five years before Simon finally found him. And we all know that witch meant harm to us."

A look passed between Trevor and Bo that I didn't like one bit.

"What is it?" I asked, clutching the bars again. "Goddammit, tell me what's going on!"

"Rafe, even if everything you say is true, it doesn't change the fact that the ridge clans are under attack from the witches. Witchcraft kept Simon from his son. If Tad really is the carrier like your witch says, that's another act against us."

"Talia can help! That's what I'm trying to tell you. You need to let me go to her. Not just because I know she's in trouble. But because she's our last best chance to stop this."

Bo dropped his head. When he lifted his eyes, they'd gone cold. "You're right. Trevor and I *don't* know what it's like to feel what the rest of you do for a fated mate. We've been denied that particular pleasure so far. So, I need you to look me in the eye and swear to me that she is what you say she is."

"Bo," I said, my voice dropping an octave. "Talia is *mine*. I've claimed her. Whether you like it or not, she's part of the McCormack clan now. She's one of us."

"Then you may not like it, but that makes the decision that much more certain," Trevor said.

"What decision?"

My chest felt hollow. That uneasy look passed between them again.

"War," Bo finally said. "We have no choice but to take the fight to the witches. It's now or never. In another few days, Simon won't be strong enough to fight and neither will Trevor. A party's forming now. We're heading down to Salt Fork."

"To do what? To wipe them out?"

"We hope it doesn't come to that," Trevor said. "But, we're taking a show of force. Either they undo this spell, or..."

"Or you're planning a massacre. Jesus Christ. And what purpose will that serve? We'll all end up dead."

"So you'd rather we just hide up here and wither away. Fuck that, Rafe. If I'm going out, I'm going out fighting."

I stepped away from the bars. Burying my face in my hands, I doubled over at the waist. It *would* be a massacre. The witches would defend themselves. We'd all seen the power they held. Good God, Talia's father could have done real damage and he was just one man. The casualties would be catastrophic on both sides. And then what? The sickness would still work its way through whoever of us was left over.

"Take me to the longhouse," I finally said. "Call another meeting."

"Rafe, it's no use," Bo said. "The vote was unanimous."

"It wasn't unanimous if I didn't cast one. The last time I checked, you can't call a full clan meeting without *all* the clans. No one speaks for Clan McCormack but me."

"It doesn't matter," Trevor said. "You're outnumbered either way. You may be their Alpha, but your clan wants to fight. Think of your father, for God's sake."

"I *am* thinking about Ansel. Fuck. It's all I've *been* thinking about. I stand to lose as much or more than all of you. And you're right, the witches started this. Or at least, one witch did. Talia didn't know for sure, but now she does. We've got to give her a chance to make her people understand. If we go in there ready to kill, there'll never be a way to take that back. The witches will fight to defend themselves and the best defense they have is that we're already compromised. If they didn't sanction this spell on Tad in the first place, they will now. Then what? You ready to kill Tad? Because right now, that's about the only thing I see that could end this, and we all know that's out of the question."

"We leave at nightfall," Bo said. He stepped around Trevor and jammed the key into the lock at the front of the cage. He pulled the cage door open, letting it clang against the opposite wall. He took a step back clearing my path toward the door.

"You're either with us or against us," Bo said. "You need to choose, Rafe. Are you loyal to the clans or the witches?"

My heart dropped. "There's no choice. You know I'm with the clans. You may not like it, but Talia *is* part of my clan now. I've claimed her as mine. No matter how much any of you hate it, you can't go against her without going against me. We've survived on this ridge longer than any other bear clans because of that one simple law. We fight together. Always. Now, call a meeting of the clans. There's another vote we need to take."

SIMON LOOKED LIKE HE'D AGED TEN YEARS IN THE FEW HOURS since I'd seen him last. I could have accepted his rage when I walked in the door. I'd earned it. No matter what the circumstances, his own son was at risk. I didn't cause it, but Talia had called it out. Like it or not, it meant she'd posed a threat to Tad. In his place, I would have acted to protect my son.

But, it wasn't rage Simon gave me as I took my place at the table. He was a man trying to do the best he could to save the people he loved. We had that in common and it tempered both of our words.

I did my best to keep my voice even and my words concise as I said my piece. Talia was part of Clan McCormack. If we went against the witches, she had to be treated differently.

"My mother said she thought your witch was trying to kill Ansel. Are you saying she's lying?" Bo asked.

I shook my head. "No. I'm saying Jenna didn't understand what was happening. Neither did I. Talia said the spell around my father fought back. That's the best way I can describe what she told me. Now, I'm telling you, I need to get to her. Every man here who's taken a mate understands the pain it causes when she's at risk. Well, Talia's at risk from her own people. She's one of us now and she's owed our protection."

Jax and Cullen put their heads together and whispered something between them. Cullen fixed a hard stare at me, but nodded when Jax slapped him on the shoulder.

"It doesn't change anything," Cullen said. "We have to act. There's no doubt that we're dying because of an attack from Talia's coven. Now you're saying she's in danger from them as well. So be it. If it comes to a fight, and I think we're all fairly certain it will, we'll do what we can to keep Talia out of it. But Rafe, if she stands with her coven against us, you have to be willing to accept the consequences."

I pressed my thumb to the bridge of my nose. I wanted to tell them I knew she wouldn't. In my heart I believed that, but I tried to put myself in her place. It was an impossible choice, one no bear had ever had to make. But, all that mattered was that I get to her. The rest would unfold as it had to.

"My loyalty is with the clans," I said. "Talia is part of my clan. Her coven isn't. If it's in her power to help us, she will. I have no doubts."

"I hope you're right," Jax said. "By God, I hope you're right. This isn't a decision that any man here has taken lightly. We have no choice. We have to take the fight to the witches. If it's as you say it is, and this was the work of one lone witch, then hopefully the coven leaders will see reason and put an end to this. If they don't, we all know what we're prepared to do."

I looked around the table. Every man gave a slow nod and a vote. "Aye."

Then all eyes turned toward me. Again, I felt my heart ripped down the middle. But, there was no question about what I had to do. I exhaled and dropped my head. "Aye."

⚜

WE LEFT AT DAYBREAK. NOT IN A THOUSAND YEARS HAD THE clans assembled in such a large number to leave Wild Ridge together. For Jax, Cullen, Simon, and me, the journey meant something different. They were leaving their mates behind. I was heading toward mine. As the only Alphas left without mates, Bo and Trevor had the luxury of pure fury. I envied them a little even as I couldn't imagine my life without Talia in it.

Heat burned me from the inside out. Talia's absence clouded my mind. The power of an *Anam Cara*'s magic was strong indeed. Without her, I didn't feel whole.

She called to me. With each mile we put behind us, the pull of her essence burned brighter within me. If I'd never set foot in the Salt Fork wilderness before, I would have found my way to her. God, she was so cold. Something restrained her. She couldn't move. She wasn't in physical pain, but a hollow space filled her heart and it didn't take long before I realized she couldn't hear me. She couldn't feel me. They'd done something to her that quieted her magic.

Hang on, my love. I called out with my mind. But, as we the day wore on and we got ever closer to the battlefield, Talia's silence took on a new, cold meaning. If she wasn't talking to me, she might not be talking to anyone. If she couldn't make the covens understand what had happened on the ridge, they wouldn't understand what we needed from them. It meant the war would have already started the second we stepped foot on coven lands.

At dusk, we reached the northern border of the witches' territory. Digby was three miles to the southeast. The green expanse of Salt Fork protected it. We'd reached the point of no return. Talia was close and the promise of her presence made my breath come short. As we reached the edge of the tree line, I doubled over, struggling to inhale.

Trevor came to me. He put a light hand on my shoulder, his eyes filled with concern. "Rafe," he said. "There's something wrong with you."

I shook my head. "It's just Talia. Being apart from her." Trevor's brow creased and he shot a look toward Simon and the others. When he looked back to me, he grabbed the collar of my shirt and forced me upright.

"You feel hot, it's hard to breathe, and you can't see straight. Rafe, look at your chest."

Cold fear snaked its way through me at Trevor's words. I didn't want to look. I didn't want it to be true. But, the minute he said it, I knew it was. I slid a hand beneath my shirt and let my fingers play along my stomach. They were there. The pox. How I'd gone so long without realizing it, I didn't know.

"It doesn't matter," I said, straightening. "It just means we've reached the point of no return. We already knew that." I gave the others a sharp nod and turned toward the woods.

It was quiet in the forest as we fanned out and headed into the deepest parts. The clans looked to me to lead the way. Instinct told me to head for the place where Talia's magic first touched mine. The cabin. Her scent still clung to the trees all around us. She'd been here recently. She'd been terrified. I closed my eyes and saw her. She'd fallen to her knees as the threat came from all around. They'd surrounded her just like the bears had done when I brought her to the ridge.

Oh, God. My Talia. It seemed no matter what, being with me brought her pain and anguish. My eyes snapped open as we reached the cabin. Was it enough? After all of it, could her people drive the truth from her heart?

"Rafe, what is it?" Simon stood at my shoulder. I hadn't realized I'd stopped. I sank to the ground, pressing my palm against the soft earth.

"She was here," I said. "They took her from this place against her will. She's close."

"Is she alive?" Trevor asked.

I nodded, but cold dread filled my stomach.

"She's very close!" I heard Talia cry out. She was behind me, then in front of me, then all around.

I spun on my heel and dropped low to the ground. A buzzing filled my head as if a wasp circled it, but there was nothing there. I looked around and all the other Alphas batted the same buzzing away from their faces.

A spell.

"They're here," Simon said. "I can feel them. I just can't fucking see them."

Trevor and Bo shifted. I shouted out a warning. Going full bear at the get-go wouldn't end well. They rose on their hind legs and roared into the trees.

The buzzing stopped and the air shimmered in front of me, making the trees go in and out of focus. Then, a sort of cleft opened. Darkness swirled around it. A blast of heat hit me in the chest and took the breath straight from my lungs. I held my ground.

A wavering figure stepped out of thin air. She wore a long, white robe and her gray hair pulled back in a bun. She had deep lines running from the corners of her mouth. She smiled at me and stepped forward. The other Alphas came to my side, but I held up a hand.

"Wait," I said. She didn't have to tell me who she was. I could sense part of Talia in her. Deep lines webbed the corners of her eyes and I saw where Talia got her part-Cherokee roots.

The woman gave me a sort of half smile then reached up and touched my face.

"I take it you're Rafe," she said.

"I am."

"Well, I'm Ellen Torre, Talia's grandmother. She said you'd come."

I put a light hand on Ellen's shoulder. She was tiny, shorter even than Talia, but with a straight back and clear eyes that she fixed on me with cold purpose.

"I wish I had better news," Ellen said. "But, son, I think you're already too late."

Chapter Fifteen

Talia

I marveled that something so simple could hold so much power. Well, not so much hold, but restrain. Toby took a considerable amount of glee in handing the shackles to his mother. Jane Winters was a formidable witch. Until today, I'd respected her above just about everyone save for my own grandmother and father. Today though, when Jane let Toby dig his fingers into my shoulders while she put those heavy steel bracelets on me, I wanted to punch her in the face.

The instant the metal cuffs closed around my wrists, I felt the fire leach out of me. My body trembled as I tried to adjust to the drop in temperature.

Lifting my wrists, I turned them, studying the welds where the shackles locked. Toby made them. And he'd done it using my father's forge. The spell that blocked my magic had to have been cast by Jane. Toby wouldn't have been powerful enough.

"I'm sorry," she said, but I didn't believe her. Gray wisps of hair floated around Jane's forehead. She kept it pulled back into a tight ponytail and it occurred to me I'd never seen her wear it down. I don't know why that mattered, but part of me struggled to reconcile what used to be normal with what was now a threat. Jane was my mother's friend. After she died, it was Jane who came to the house first bringing casseroles and helping Grandma Torre clean the house. Now, she looked at me with fear and a fair amount of disgust. I didn't want to hate her. I reminded myself she was ignorant, just like the others.

"Where's my father?" I asked for the dozenth time. After the coven had surrounded us at the cabin, they led him away from me. He'd yelled to me not to worry even though we both knew we had every reason to.

"Garrett's been trying to plead your case for the better part of the morning."

"Why aren't you?"

Toby stepped between us. His hand curled into a fist and I felt the menace pouring off of him. Some detached part of my brain reminded me what Rafe had said about him. He meant to do me harm. He had evil inside of him. God, why hadn't I ever sensed it before?

"Toby," Jane said, her tone sharp. "Wait outside. I'll call you if I need anything else."

"I'm not leaving you alone with her," he said. "We don't know what she's capable of."

I held up my shackled wrists. "What, you don't trust your own handiwork? That's not saying much for your mother's powers or your smithing abilities."

When Toby raised his fist, I flinched. Jane put a hand over his and shoved him backward. "No," she said. "Not that way, Toby. Talia's going to have to face up to what she's done with the coven. It's not up to us to decide."

A tiny line of perspiration broke out along Toby's brow. Clenching his jaw hard, he finally stepped away. Jane nodded to him and he left the room. We were in the old library, but all the spellbooks had been taken out. Because of it, the magic shackles seemed like overkill. The coven had ensorcelled the building long ago to prevent any witch from using magic on another witch in here. It was supposed to be a safe place. I felt anything but.

"This is wrong, Jane. Everything about this is wrong. You of all people should understand why." Jane stood against the wall with her hands crossed in front of her. A tiny line of worry creased her forehead.

"Don't you dare try and pass judgment on me," she finally said.

I couldn't help the wry smile that came. "Are you kidding me? I'm not allowed to pass judgment on you, but it's fine if you judge me? Jane, you were there when my aunt died. You saw firsthand the hate in her heart she had for those bear shifters."

I didn't say the other thing that came to mind, but it hung between us. That day we went to try and bring my Aunt Gwendolyn back into the fold, it had been Jane's power that finally stopped her. I'd only been there for the blood connection. Lori, the other witch with us, was nowhere near as strong as Jane was. In the end, it had been *Jane's* fire magic that had dealt the lethal blow to my aunt. I didn't blame her for it. We had no choice. I felt the malevolence of my aunt's magic. She would have killed us all if she'd been strong enough. But of the two of us, Jane Winters had posed the most recent direct threat to another witch.

Jane pushed her shoulder off the wall and came toward me. "Your Aunt Gwendolyn was a lot of things, but she knew the kind of risk shifters pose to us, Talia. In her own warped way, she was trying to protect us. I don't condone her actions. But, I understand them a hell of a lot better than I understand yours."

"You understand nothing. And I'd like to see my father."

"You're not in a position to demand anything. The coven's gathered outside."

"The *whole* coven?" I swallowed hard. Here in the library with Toby's magic shackles and the damper surrounding the entire building, I couldn't sense them at first. Now, I made myself still and quiet, slowing my breathing. I could hear them now. It reached me like a distant hum or a swarm of bees. They were out there. The entire coven. And they were here for me.

A sharp knock on the door made me jump. Jane scowled and walked backward toward the door so she could keep her eyes on me the whole time. My God, I had no idea what she thought I could do to her. She cracked the door open, keeping one eye on me.

I couldn't hear what she said or see who was on the other side of the door. But, when Jane's face fell and she gave a curt nod, my heart sank. They were ready for me. I had no idea what to expect, but whatever happened next, it would be in front of the entire North American Circean coven.

Jane motioned toward me. It occurred to me to wonder what she'd do if I just flat out refused to go with her. Maybe the smartest thing to do would be to stay right where I was. If any of the coven were planning to harm me, they couldn't do it here in the library. This was probably the safest place I could be right now.

The idea had merit except for one thing. I wanted to see my father. He'd risked his life to follow me to Wild Ridge, both from the bear clans and the coven itself. Sure, my transgressions with

Rafe were worse, but my dad broke just about every other rule we had venturing into bear country. He'd been brave enough to come after me. I wouldn't cower behind these walls. Plus, there was the practical problem of starving to death in here.

Jane stood in the doorway. I slowly rose to my feet. Holding my shackled hands in front of me, I straightened my back and walked outside.

The population of Digby, Ohio seemed to have tripled. They'd gathered in an abandoned field directly across from the library. At first, I didn't recognize a soul. Hundreds upon hundreds of witches stood in a semicircle, their gazes all turned toward the doorway of the old schoolhouse. My breath hitched and the courage I'd summoned seemed to evaporate into a puddle of sweat that trickled down my back. But, I heard only a rumble of murmurs from the crowd. Nobody picked up rocks to throw at me...yet. I blinked hard and hoped that was a good sign. I just prayed these people came here to listen.

I descended the schoolhouse steps and headed straight for the crowd. I kept my head held high as Jane walked at my side. I searched frantically for my father. He had to be here somewhere. I could draw strength from his steady gaze and kind eyes.

Jane led me through the crowd. They'd erected a small aluminum platform. I found it almost comical. It was the same one we used during local election campaigns. In the summer months, the mayoral candidates would stand at makeshift podiums and debate in front of the crowd. Our current mayor, Mona Mattingly, stood at the edge of the platform with a dour expression and downcast eyes.

Jane stepped around me and went to Mayor Mattingly's side. They were joined by Jack Quinn, the town sheriff, and Jean and Connor Anderson, the gas station owners. The five of them represented the coven elders of Digby. Though the coven would decide things as a group, the opinion of the Five held great weight. My heart sank. Jane Winters was already against me. Jean and Conner Anderson wouldn't meet my eyes.

I let out a breath and turned toward the crowd. A disturbance in the front row drew my attention. After some pushing and shoving, my father burst through the line. He looked as if he'd aged ten years since the last time I saw him, and I realized he likely had. I raised my bound wrists and tried to put on a brave face. I gave him a smiling wink then turned toward the Five.

"Am I going to be given a chance to speak for myself?" I said, raising my voice so they could hear me several rows back. A gasp rose from the crowd. Maybe it was a sign of disrespect, but I needed some sense of control.

Mona put up a silencing hand and walked toward me. "Your father's been speaking quite a bit on your behalf. But, we still have questions. Are you willing to answer truthfully?"

"I swear on my mother's soul that everything I say here will be the truth as I know it."

My father's head dropped and Mona nodded.

"Do you deny that you've conspired and consorted with the bear shifters?" Mona asked.

The question took me aback. "Conspired? I don't know what you mean by that. I've done nothing against the coven."

"You harbored a bear shifter in secret, on coven lands."

I opened my mouth to answer, but no sound would come out. I took another breath and tried again. "That part is true. But I had a good reason. It was an accident, but I hurt that bear. The night

CURSE OF THE BEARS

I declared, he caught me by surprise. So, I made sure he was healed."

"She's lying!" Toby stepped forward. "Or she's only telling you half the truth. She's lain with that bear. I saw her. I've shown you all the proof. He knows who we are and where we live. God knows how else she's betrayed us to the bear clans."

"Stop!" I shouted. "All of you need to wake up. Yes, I went to Wild Ridge with him. There's sickness there. A spell has been cast against the shifters by one of us. They're dying at our hands, and if you think they won't try to put up a fight, you're all fooling yourselves. They're going to come. I can promise you that. We owe them our help if you want to avoid a Shifter War that will decimate the coven."

"She has no proof of any of this!" Jane shouted me down. "Toby is the only one of us who has shown real proof of what Talia's done."

"Dad," I turned to him. "You were there. You *saw* that bear cub. Did you tell them?"

My father pushed his way to the platform. He jumped up to stand beside me. His shoulder brushed mine in a gesture of solidarity that melted my heart. "I told them," he said. "But they're too stubborn to listen."

"You want more proof?" I said. Mona clutched the library's spell-books in front of her. The small black volume poked out in the middle of the stack. I raised my wrists and pointed to it.

"Look inside the dark book," I demanded. "You'll see. There's a spell missing on the final pages. There's black magic at work, and I'm not the source of it. It was my Aunt Gwendolyn. It's why she kept that bear cub away from his family."

Mona's eyes widened and the Connors recoiled. Speaking my aunt's name in front of the coven was forbidden. I was just so damn tired of rules. Bears were dying and because of their stubborn minds and old prejudices, they were willing to ignore it to their own detriment.

To her credit, Mona at least shuffled the books and opened the dark one to the last pages. Color drained from her face as she saw what I had and its meaning sank in. She snapped her eyes to mine.

"And you expect us to believe *you* weren't the one that took this spell?"

"I'm right here!" I yelled. "Why in the world would I tell you the spell was missing in the first place and give you one more thing to hold against me while I'm standing here powerless in front of a few hundred witches?"

"I saw the boy," my father said. "I've told you that already. That poor bear shifter is covered in something mystical. He's an innocent. I just thank God that whatever it is doesn't seem to affect him."

"He's a carrier," I explained. "My aunt must have worked that magic on him. She must have always known his family would find him and send him straight back to Wild Ridge."

The Andersons looked horrified. Fat tears rolled down Mrs. Anderson's cheeks. Jane and Jack Quinn didn't seem convinced. They looked at me with renewed contempt. I'd sown the first seeds of doubt in Mona's mind. I could feel it.

But two seconds later, none of it mattered anymore.

My heart thundered in my chest and a pain so fierce spread through me it drove me to my knees. Dad tried to catch me, but I dropped like a stone.

Screams rose in the crowd and a howling wind rose. Lightning streaked across the sky as the tension among the fire mages

CURSE OF THE BEARS

threatened to erupt. If I'd had more time, maybe I could have talked the witches down. But time ran out as all eyes turned toward the hilltop above us.

My grandmother stood atop it, holding her gnarled walking stick in front of her. She only used it when it rained, and today, the storm of the millennium had started to brew. Behind her, at least two dozen bears rose on their hind legs. One by one, they let loose a primal growl that echoed through the valley. Oh, God. Grandma. No matter what else happened here today, she'd taken a tremendous risk leading the bears to us. She'd cloaked them, otherwise the coven would have sensed them long before they got within sight of us. My heart burst with love for Grandma Torre at the same time sobering fear for her safety made my blood run cold.

"Hold!" Mona shouted. "Nobody move!"

I couldn't tell if she was talking to the coven, or the bears. Neither group listened. The witches began to scatter and the bears charged down the hill.

My father got his hands beneath my arms and helped me to my feet. I'd have given anything to be able to break the shackles binding me. I wanted desperately to call to my fire. I felt powerless against whatever might come.

One bear broke the line and ran ahead of the others. I knew him right away. Rafe called him Bo. He skidded to a halt just before the steps to the platform. He dropped to all fours and opened his jaw as he growled. The force of it blew Mona Mattingly's hair back. Every pair of eyes in the crowd except for mine focused on the awesome power of the gigantic grizzly in their midst. But, I looked behind him. Heat flooded my senses and my heart stopped.

The crowd parted one last time and Rafe stepped forward. How he'd kept his bear in check while the others let out that primal roar I'll never know. But, he stood tall and proud, his dark eyes shining as he turned toward the Five. My chest rose and fell with heavy breaths and the air went still as Rafe took the steps to the platform in one agile leap.

"My name is Rafe McCormack. I'm Alpha to my clan and speak for them. Talia is my mate and part of that clan. If any one of you touches a hair on her head, you'll have to answer to the rest of Wild Ridge and me."

My breath caught in my throat and it took everything in me not to run into Rafe's arms. But I could sense the shift in the coven. Their collective, gathering power could be deadly. I didn't move; I could scarcely breathe. Finally, it was Mona who broke the silence.

"You aren't welcome here. We've kept the peace between your kind and ours for twelve hundred years. Your careless actions and those of Talia have threatened us to the brink of war. I'm going to ask you once to leave of your own accord."

"There's no peace," I said. "There's no peace because the bears of Wild Ridge are suffering because of *our* magic. If you truly serve justice, then the coven owes Wild Ridge a debt. We have to find a way to undo what's been done to them."

"You've proven nothing, Talia. And your opinion is compromised. I don't know what this bear has done to you, but you aren't acting in the coven's interest."

I felt Rafe's bear stir. The growl he held inside vibrated through the floor and went straight up my spine. I wanted desperately to go to him. I needed to feel his strength. It fueled my own. But, when I looked at him again, something was wrong.

He stood with his fists curled at his side, his feet apart, and he leaned slightly forward. His body wavered as if the wind could unsteady him. His dark eyes clouded over and the heat coming from him seemed hot enough to singe my hair. I went to him.

Mona called out a warning, but I couldn't heed it. I took three steps toward Rafe and his strength seemed to drain from him. Bo let out another growl of warning, but it was too late. Rafe keeled over with the majestic grace of an oak tree.

The crowd gasped as Rafe fell to his knees. I dropped beside him and raised my hands to touch his face. He was burning up.

"Dad, help me!" I cried. My father seemed to know exactly what to do. Rafe flinched when my father's hands grabbed the collar of his shirt. He ripped it open, exposing Rafe's skin. My shaking hands hovered over his broad back. His flesh was covered in the telltale pox marks of the sickness the others had died from.

"Why didn't you tell me?" I whispered, tears spilling freely.

Rafe's ragged breaths sent terror through me. He shook his head. Trying to focus through hooded lids, he staggered back to his feet. My father and I got his arms over our shoulders and helped him stand upright as he faced the Five.

"Do you see?" I spoke for him. "Come closer if you don't. One touch and you'll know what I know. This sickness is magic-borne. For God's sake, if you value the peace our ancestors died for, you owe them at least the benefit of the doubt."

I thought they'd argue with me. But all five of them, the Andersons, Jack Quinn, Mona, and even Jane formed a circle around us. Jane touched Rafe first. She locked hands with Mona. Their magic hummed between them. Jane's was fire-based; Mona's was wind. A thin electric spark lit the air around Rafe. I kept a steady hand on his chest. I knew his bear recoiled against the presence of so many witches. But, he trusted me. It lasted only a few seconds, but it seemed like hours.

Finally, the Five stepped away from Rafe. His step faltered and my father and I had to strain to keep him upright. I shot a look to Bo's bear. He paced and chuffed at the base of the platform. The rest of the clans formed a perimeter of threat around the gathered coven.

Jane took the black spellbook from Mona. The Five closed ranks, forming a circle with their backs to us. I could feel the hum of their magic and for just a sliver of time, I felt renewed hope. But, when they finally broke and Jane stepped forward, the look on her face was grave.

"You're right," she said. "This is a very dark spell. Bear, you have my word this was not sanctioned by this coven. The only witch alive who has willingly broken our treaty with you is Talia."

"Talia's done nothing wrong," he whispered. "And I give you my word, if you harm a hair on her head, you'll answer to the clans."

"So you believe me? You understand what has to happen? We have to make this right," I said.

Mona took a great breath and let it out with a sigh. Her expression softened as she came to me. She put a maternal hand on my cheek that made Rafe emit a low, threatening growl.

"You were right about all of it, Talia. This magic was taken without permission and it came from that book. It has Gwendolyn's mystical fingerprints all over it."

My heart sank. As much as I'd suspected it all along, there was a piece missing. "Then how is this sickness still spreading? How is that poor bear cub still carrying it within him? Gwendolyn's dead. Her spells should have dissipated with her last breath."

I felt my father's weight shift. He went rigid on the other side of Rafe. A look passed between him and Jane that sent a cold spear of terror through me.

"Blood magic," he said.

"What?"

"She found a way to bond her spell with blood magic," Jane said. "It probably didn't even take effect *until* she died. Oh, God. It means that we...that I..."

"An insurance policy," Rafe said through gritted teeth. "In case we got to her."

"I'm afraid so," Mona said.

A part of me could feel sorry for Jane. She looked like she was going to be sick. If Aunt Gwendolyn's spell didn't take effect until the moment she died, Jane herself had unwittingly set it in motion.

"So, fine," I said. "We know what it is; there has to be a way to counter it now."

My father let go of Rafe. He doubled over at the waist and covered his mouth with his hand. He looked ready to vomit.

"Talia," Jane said, tears filling her eyes. "The only way to counter blood magic is with a blood sacrifice."

Her mouth made words. My ears listened, but I couldn't hear. I couldn't make out any meaning. Rafe stiffened beside me. His chest heaved with racking coughs. I felt his heart's erratic beat. He was so sick. The virus was growing in strength. It had taken his father days to get this bad and he was older and weaker to start with. Rafe was one of the strongest Alphas in the clans.

My father straightened. His eyes went flat and he wouldn't look at me as he walked in front of me. He squared his shoulders and faced the Five.

"Then it should be me," he said. "Gwendolyn was my sister. This falls on me."

There was no more discussion. The skies darkened and the first drops of rain began to fall. My ears started to ring. I didn't understand what was happening. My brain seemed to fight processing what my eyes were seeing.

The Five fanned out, forming a line in front of my father. They joined hands with Jane in the center. To her credit, she at least looked horrified at what was about to happen. There was no discussion. No vote. Just swift action and resolve. Everything seemed to spiral out of control.

No.

That single word formed in my brain. I couldn't feel my heartbeat. I couldn't hear the words coming out of Rafe's mouth beside me. My father looked back over his shoulder and mouthed, "I love you."

Swirling color materialized in front of the five witches as each of them drew on the Source. Spokes on a wheel. Earth. Water. Air. Fire. Blood magic. Oh, God. My father's blood.

The world stopped. I reacted. As a column of white light came up from the ground, I let go of Rafe. He called my name. I felt him, but he couldn't stop me. Blood magic. Blood sacrifice.

No!

As the white light gathered strength and changed direction, I threw myself in front of my father. I didn't deliberate or think. Instinct compelled me. I would protect those I loved. Blood magic. A life for a life. The bolt hit me first in the chest, then my hair caught fire. The magic holding the shackles together let loose and the last thing I saw before I hit the ground was an explosion of metal as they broke apart.

Chapter Sixteen

RAFE

Talia died. When her heart stopped, it hit me like a hammer blow. Through rage and fever and fire, my bear rose up. I ripped at my chest and went to my knees.

The witches' light burned a crater into the flimsy platform and scorched the ground beneath us. At first, I couldn't see her. I thought the earth had opened up and swallowed her. I heard her father's anguished cry as I slid down into twisted metal and went to her.

Talia lay in a fetal position, her dark hair turned white at the crown. So deep was my grief that I couldn't feel the sickness leaving me. Later, others would tell me that the sores on my flesh vanished in the blink an eye. The same thing happened to Simon and Trevor. Deep inside me, I felt another weight lift as far away, I sensed my father's bear call to me, strong, healed, and full of fury. It didn't matter. I'd suffer a thousand deaths to take just this one away.

The clans came down from the hilltop. I didn't care if they ripped every witch to shreds. I didn't care if the witches burned each of them to the ground in that single moment. All that mattered was how cold Talia's skin felt as I gathered her into my arms.

I kissed her. Her lips had turned white and when her head rolled back, her eyes were open. Those beautiful green eyes had turned silver.

"Baby," I whispered. "Talia. I love you."

I kissed her again. I heard rumbling behind me. In some detached corner of my brain I wondered whether the shifters and the witches really were tearing each other apart. But, I didn't care. They could rip me to shreds next. For now, I just wanted to hold my love.

The skies opened up and thunder rained down. Rain pelted my back and soaked Talia's body. I rocked her in my arms and it seemed God Himself railed against the loss of my beloved.

Then, the rain stopped. The world spun and I came back into myself.

The coven surrounded me. Talia's father's grief-stricken face swam in front of me. He tried to get to her. I was trapped between beast and man. My vision grew dark as I saw the world through the bear's eyes even as I stayed on my feet. I let out a low, threatening growl, ready to rip anyone to shreds...bear or witch...who tried to get between Talia and me.

"I'll kill you for this," I said to the coven elders. They took slow steps backward. "I promised you'd answer to the clans if you hurt her."

"Rafe," Bo said. I snapped at him and he too took a step back.

"Don't, son," Talia's father choked out his words. "Don't make her sacrifice mean nothing."

He said other things. I could hear none of them. I could only feel the bottomless grief rising up to tear me apart. I leaned over Talia again, drawing her to me. I lifted my head to the sky and a growl ripped from my throat, strong enough to shake the ground beneath us.

I sobbed into Talia's hair. This was wrong. This couldn't be. I promised her I'd never let anything hurt her as long as I had breath in my body. It didn't matter that she'd made the choice herself. I failed her. I was never worthy of her in the first place.

Time stood still and the world spun as I held her in my arms and questioned God. Then, as suddenly as it started, the world stopped spinning and everything went still.

A single breath. One beat. Then two. As lightning cracked no more than a few feet away from me, Talia blinked. Her skin grew warm in my arms and her back arched as she sucked in a great, heaving breath.

"Talia! Baby?"

She coughed and sputtered, expelling a blue mist from her lungs. Then, she rolled over in my arms and gripped my shoulders. When she looked up at me, her eyes filled with wonder. They were green again.

"Rafe?" she said. "Did it work?"

I opened my mouth to answer, but found I was speechless. Water dripped from my hair and Talia started to shiver. Soaked to the bone, her clothes clung to her. But, she was strong. Her heart beat steady and her pulse joined mine.

"What happened?" she said as I helped her to her feet. With my arms around her, we made our way out of the tangled wreckage of the platform.

We were greeted by the shocked stares of hundreds of pairs of eyes. The witches' council stepped forward. Talia's father pushed them aside and went to her. I kept a hand on her back but let her go to him. He sobbed into her hair as I leveled my gaze at the witches.

The oldest, the one Talia called Mona, got brave enough to come near me. She leaned down and peered into Talia's face. Her own split into a smile as she put a hand on Talia's forehead, touched her shoulder, and pressed a hand to Talia's chest.

"What the hell happened?" Talia asked.

"I don't know," Mona answered.

"That was blood magic," the one called Jane said. "Your blood for Gwendolyn's. And it worked. Are you healed, bear? Is the sickness out of you?"

I put my arms in front of me and felt my back for pox. I found none. I took in a great breath of air and my lungs felt clear. Simon emerged from the crowd looking clear-eyed and healthy. Beside him, Trevor looked strong and whole.

"I think so," I said.

"Blood magic," Mona said, she had a wide grin that almost bordered on crazy.

"Mona?" Talia asked.

"Blood magic!" she said again. "One life in exchange for another."

"Right. You said that. So, I should be dead."

"Goddammit, Talia!" Her father shook her once. My protective inner bear growled, but Garrett Lear's paternal consternation seemed just as powerful. "Why the hell did you do that?"

"I don't know," she answered. "I just reacted. I wasn't going to stand there and let them kill you for something that wasn't your fault."

"Talia," Mona said. "You mean you don't sense it yet?"

"Sense what?"

Something was happening. I didn't like it. Mona was too close to her. Her expression too crazed.

"One life," she said again. "You need *one* life to break the circle of a blood spell. These are natural rules, Talia. The Source cannot take two."

Two. Mona said it again. I felt Talia's heartbeat quicken. I put an arm around her. Her mouth dropped open and she put a hand on her stomach. Something flickered in her eyes. I stepped in front of her and put my hands on her shoulders.

"Talia?"

She shook her head. Her eyes flashed with some secret knowledge and misted with tears. Smiling, she took my hand and slowly guided it over hers where she pressed it against her womb.

One life. Not two. The world slowed as I closed my eyes and listened for it. One heartbeat. Mine. A second heartbeat. Talia's. But below that, faint as a whisper, I felt the third heartbeat.

My eyes snapped open. Talia's bright smile melted me.

"Rafe," she smiled.

"Yes, my love?"

"Take me home."

Laughing, I picked Talia up and twirled her in my arms. A cheer erupted from the crowd. The coven was still uneasy with the bears in their midst, but they seemed genuinely happy with

Talia's triumph. It was all of our triumphs. My brave, beautiful Talia.

I set her down and put an arm around her. I wasn't sure I could ever let her go again. Her father looked at me. Talia's grandmother had come down from the hilltop and put a gentle hand on his shoulder.

"Leave them be, Garrett," she said. "They've earned a little bit of peace."

A look passed between Garrett Lear and me. I gave him a solemn nod. He entrusted Talia to me. I put a hand out and shook his. We couldn't pretend things would be easy between us; we had too much history to overcome. But, for today, we'd chipped away at a little of the prejudice that kept us apart. For now, it would have to be enough.

As the clans closed ranks around us, Talia and I made our way through the crowd. I would take her home, to Wild Ridge. My love. My mate. My *Anam Cara*. And the tiny life we'd created inside her that had been strong enough to save us all.

We took the first steps toward our new life together. But, Talia stopped. She gave me a grim nod and pulled away from me.

"What is it?" I asked.

"I can't leave yet. There's one more thing I have to do."

She turned on her heel and walked away from me. She went to the edge of the platform where Toby stood beside his mother.

Talia squared her shoulders. Quick as a flash, she drew back a fist and landed a punch straight across the bridge of Toby's nose. He staggered sideways and blinked wildly as blood spurted down his chin. He landed on his ass, shaking the stars out of his eyes.

Talia stood over him, blue light sparking from her hands. "If you ever lay a hand on another woman, Toby Winters, a broken nose will be the least of your problems."

Smiling, I put my arm around Talia's waist and kissed her cheek. "Come on, baby" I said. "Let's get the hell out of here."

She shook her hand, the knuckles had already started to swell, but I recognized good pain when I saw it. Talia turned and winked at her father, then we headed north toward home.

Epilogue

TALIA

Six Weeks Later...

"You're sure?"

I rolled to my back and threaded my fingers behind my head. The sun-dappled leaves of an oak tree shimmered above us. High on the ridge, the cool, blue waters of Lake Superior churned below us. I didn't think I'd ever grow tired of this view. The fresh air intoxicated me as I took a deep breath and rolled to my side.

"I'm sure," I said for the millionth time. "He's not even as big as your thumb, yet."

Rafe lifted his hand and flexed said thumb. Then, he reached for me, gently grasping my nipple and rolling it until it pebbled for him. I felt the instant flare of heat between my legs. God, how did he do that? Just a look or a touch and my body rose to meet his.

"And you're sure it's a he?" he asked, again for the millionth time.

KIMBER WHITE

"Mmm. I really am. And don't ask me why again. I know because I know."

"Will he be like you or like me?"

I caressed Rafe's jaw, loving the feel of his strong bones, beneath my fingertips. Leaning forward I kissed him.

"Maybe he'll be like both of us."

"Wouldn't that be something? A shifter-witch."

"Or a witch-shifter. But no, and of course we won't know for sure until he's here and he's older. But, I think his magic is strictly earthbound, my love. Strong. Virile. An Alpha, just like his daddy."

"Well, then God help us in about twelve years."

I snorted as I laughed and Rafe pulled me close to him again. His body molded to mine and I felt him rise for me. It had been less than an hour since the last time we made love. But, already we both felt the need again.

Rafe went to his back. His cock sprang free, pointing toward the sky. Smiling, I shimmied down the length of him, eager to use the newest skill I'd learned. I circled my tongue around his shaft, loving the salty taste of him and the way he seemed to melt beneath me. I took slow, languid strokes, enjoying the velvety thickness of his erection. He was heavy and full for me when I cupped his balls and stroked them.

Rising, I smiled as I saw the look of contentment wash over him. I shifted my weight and stretched along the length of him.

"I love you, bear" I whispered.

"You better," he said, erupting in a low, wicked laugh. "You're certainly trouble, witch."

"I'm trouble? Are you kidding? You're one hell of a handful, mister." To prove my point, I cupped his balls again and gave them a gentle tug that made Rafe moan.

He rolled to his side and kissed me. "I love you more."

Swinging my leg over his hip, I straddled him. Rafe settled to his back again and hooked his fingers behind his head, enjoying the view. Giggling, I slid down, seating myself over his turgid length. Oh, God. He was full and hard and mine. I fit around him perfectly, loving the gentle stretch as I took him in all the way down to the root.

We were slow with each other then. Taking our time to enjoy the feel of each other's bodies. I traced my fingers along his hard curves. I took him deep as he slid his hands over the slope of my hips. I loved the way he gently grasped my nipples when he felt me quicken.

I rode him with abandon; throwing my head back I focused on how full he made me feel both in body and in soul. He was mine, I was his. I could scarcely believe there was ever a time when I doubted it.

Fate. Soulmates. *Anam Cara*.

I came hard and deep. Rafe waited for me. With a firm grip on my hips, he drove himself home. Then he exploded inside of me as light shot from my fingertips and the world spun. His low laughter brought me back into myself and I realized I'd done it again. We were suspended a few feet off the ground as the crescendo of my orgasm reached its peak. Slowly, carefully, I brought us back down to earth.

When I slid off of him, Rafe gathered me close and kissed the top of my head. "I don't think I'm ever going to get tired of that."

I kissed him back. "Good. Because I don't think I'm ever going to be able to control it."

This made him laugh again. I ran my thumb across the broad planes of his cheekbones. My bear. My love. We'd stay out here in the wilderness until the stars came out. His magic would call to mine. Later, he'd shift and I'd marvel at the strength of his power. But for now, something else gnawed at me. I didn't want to spoil the mood with questions, but it seemed the time was right.

"Do you think they'll ever trust me?"

Rafe smiled. I hadn't asked him this before, but he knew exactly what I meant. "I could ask you the same thing."

I bit my lip. "My father already does. He knows you were willing to give your life for mine. Since you have that in common, it's earned you a fair amount of brownie points. And Grandma just wants me to be happy. She knows you make me happy."

He smoothed a lock of hair away from my face. I had a white streak along the crown now. Rafe twirled it between his fingertips. "Well," he finally said. "If you ever need it, this is a pretty good reminder of the fact that you pretty much actually *did* die to save them. I'd say that earns *you* a fair amount of brownie points. I'm not saying the bear clans are going to start an annual hug-a-witch day over it, but they'll accept you as one of us. They already have."

I pressed my forehead against his chest, loving his scent. Rafe's essence was the wilderness around us and his own manly smell.

"And they'll accept him, too," Rafe said. He leaned forward and put a gentle kiss on my stomach.

One life. A bridge between Rafe's kind and mine.

I knew we had a long way to go, witches and shifters. Old wounds were hard to heal. But maybe, just maybe, we'd taken the first important steps to putting the past behind us. It was clear to me now how much our people needed each other. There was a path forward and I believed in my heart that Rafe and I were meant to start down it for all of us. If a spell had wiped out the female shifters, maybe another one would bring them back. Maybe there were others like me whose magic was bound to the shifters as mine was. It would be hard, I knew. There would be setbacks. But most of all, we had hope and one last thing that might be stronger than everything else.

I kissed my love again. His eyes sparkled as he looked at me. "What are you thinking about, baby?"

Smiling, I threaded my fingers through his and snuggled into the warm space where I fit best, pressing my cheek to the hollow of his shoulder.

"Magic, my love. Magic."

Rafe's low, sultry laugh sent heat skittering through me and desire made me rise to him again. It would be magic indeed that would save us both. Later, as Rafe held me close the stars came out and seemed to sparkle just for us.

Magic indeed.

A Note from Kimber White

I hope you enjoyed the ride with Rafe and Talia. In some ways, I had more fun writing this book than just about any other. I have a feeling we haven't seen the last of the Circean coven.

Up next, the last two bachelor Alphas on Wild Ridge will finally get their story told in Last of the Bears. Bo and Trevor will have the battle to end all battles to win the woman they both love. This is a love triangle of epic proportions when a female shifter finds her way on Wild Ridge lands.

If you're new to the Wild Ridge Bears series and would like to know about Simon's son Tad and what happened with Talia's mysterious Aunt Gwen, check out Rebel of the Bears.

For a first look at my next new release, sign up for my newsletter today. You'll be the first to know about my new releases and special discounts available only to subscribers. You'll also get a FREE EBOOK right now, as a special welcome gift for joining. I promise not to spam you, share your email or engage in other general assholery. You can unsubscribe anytime you like (I'll only cry a little). You can sign up here! http://www.kimberwhite.com/newsletter-signup

Psst . . . can I ask you a favor?

If you liked this story, can you do something for me? Please consider leaving a review. Reviews help authors like me stay visible and allow me to keep bringing you more stories. Reviews are the fuel that keeps us going. Please and thank you.

And if you STILL want more, I'd love to hang out with you on Facebook. I like to share story ideas, casting pics, and general insanity on a daily basis.

From the bottom of my heart though, THANK YOU for your support. You rock hard.

See you on the wild side!

Kimber

KimberWhite.com

kimberwhiteauthor@gmail.com

Books by Kimber White

Wild Ridge Bears Series

Lord of the Bears (featuring Jaxson)

Outlaw of the Bears (featuring Cullen)

Rebel of the Bears (featuring Simon)

Curse of the Bears (Featuring Rafe)

Last of the Bears (Featuring Bo and Trevor)

Wild Lake Wolves Series

Rogue Alpha

Dark Wolf

Primal Heat

Savage Moon

Hunter's Heart

Wild Hearts (Prequel featuring Pat Bonner)

Claimed by the Pack (Wolf Shifter Series)

The Alpha's Mark

Sweet Submission

Rising Heat

Pack Wars

Choosing an Alpha

Mammoth Forest Wolves